He Didn't Mind Danger

Books by Michael Gilbert
available in Perennial Library

AFTER THE FINE WEATHER

BE SHOT FOR SIXPENCE

BLOOD AND JUDGMENT

CLOSE QUARTERS

THE COUNTRY-HOUSE BURGLAR

THE DANGER WITHIN

DEATH HAS DEEP ROOTS

FEAR TO TREAD

HE DIDN'T MIND DANGER

PETRELLA AT Q

TROUBLE

He
Didn't Mind
Danger

Michael Gilbert

PERENNIAL LIBRARY

Harper & Row, Publishers, New York
Cambridge, Grand Rapids, Philadelphia, St. Louis
San Francisco, London, Singapore, Sydney, Tokyo

This book was originally published in 1948 in Great Britan by Hodder & Stoughton Ltd. under the title *They Never Looked Inside*. It was first published in the United States by Harper & Row, Publishers.

First PERENNIAL LIBRARY edition.

LIBRARY OF CONGRESS CATALOG CARD NUMBER 88-45959
ISBN 0-06-080964-7

89 90 91 92 93 WB/OPM 10 9 8 7 6 5 4 3 2 1

Contents

1

Prologue with Violence

A thin streak of grey across the darkness.

The complete stillness of suspended animation. The stillness of held breath. The stillness of checked movement; and round it the darkness.

It was a cold blackness, but dusty, and Rod was plagued with the fear that he might break into the father and mother of all sneezes. He was watching the thin grey streak, as he had been watching it now for the past five minutes. It seemed like hours. The streak was vertical, not horizontal, and it represented the edge of a door standing two inches ajar. The door was at the top of a flight of stairs which ran down from the first floor to the half-landing. And the greyness was all that was left, at that distance and infiltration, of the electric light in the basement room where the caretaker sat.

A glow-worm came and went ten feet away, and Rod guessed that "Gunner" was using his pencil-torch with discretion. There followed an interminable period of scratching. (Lock picking was all very well, he reflected, when done in the comfort and security of the back room, with friends to quiz and applaud. Even when you were blindfolded and had to work by guess and by God with a stop watch against you.)

1

A loud snap—the "lifter" had slipped again.

His thoughts ran on.

That was It. This was the real thing. This was a job. Which made things both easier and more difficult. More interesting, certainly. In the sixteen years of life he had never known anything to touch it.

Another snap—disastrously loud. Gunner was certainly off form. It was Sunday night. No, wrong again, it must be Monday morning by now, and getting on, too. Without shifting his position he looked down at the watch on his thin wrist. The luminous paint was chipped and worn but he was able from practice to make it out. Half-past three already.

For some seconds now Gunner had been silent. The torch was out, so presumably he was using both hands, one for the "lifter" and one for the "shifter". Came a slurring sound quite unlike anything which had gone before, followed by a soft click.

Good; that meant the office door would open. Here it came, throwing a widening band of yellow down the passage. Rod was disconcerted for a moment, then remembered that the full moon must have swung over their heads during the hours they had sat in the darkness.

He could see Gunner quite plainly, outlined against the window, moving from side to side. He was working quietly, opening the drawers of the big desk.

The temptation became too much for Rod. He knew that his job was to stay by the landing door: but surely —the old fool in the basement must be asleep over his gas fire by now. He hadn't made a move for more than three hours.

Rod moved into the office, stooping first, as he had been taught, to sight the furniture against the window. As he came up to Gunner's elbow the pencil light came on again for a moment and he heard his companion draw in his breath.

"Got it."

A thin key, but in the one glance unmistakably a safe key. The little torch came into play again on the great flat green door of the safe, as Gunner, with his thick, workmanlike fingers, slid up the cover plate of the lock.

Two keyholes presented themselves, set like the hands of a clock showing twenty minutes to eleven.

Gunner slipped the key into the lower slot and pressed upwards.

Nothing happened.

He tried again—then, suddenly, put out all his surprising strength.

Rod saw the thin shank of the key bending and cried a warning.

Unconsciously both man and boy had dropped their former furtiveness and silence and were moving with an almost contemptuous freedom. The torch was never off now. Again, and then again Gunner bent and twisted the key. The sweat was pouring from the palms of his hands.

"Let me try," said Rod.

He took the key right out, waited for a moment and then slid it back. It went home with such a true, sweet feel that he knew it must be the right one. But shift it would not.

Then, as clearly as if they had been spoken behind his shoulder, the words came to him—"Never pull against the handle. Let the handle do its own work."

He was cooler than Gunner now.

"Put your weight on the handle," he said. "No, put your gloves on first." The man pulled a pair of woollen gloves out of his pocket.

"Try it upwards."

As Gunner tugged the great brass handle it moved

appreciably. The key came through with a soft slurring noise and the safe door swung back.

It was at this precise moment that they heard the steps coming up the stairs.

Rod was frozen—only his stomach seemed to turn right over.

The footsteps were slow and unhurried.

Something registered in Rod's brain and life flowed on again. It was the watchman, no doubt of that, but he hadn't heard them. If he had heard them he wouldn't be moving in that particular unhurried way. There was no time to shut the safe, so it had to be—the other thing.

His feet had carried him quietly back to his position behind the landing door.

He could hear the complaining whine and grunt of the old man's breath as he came up the last flight. Grey streak had turned to yellow. He was carrying a torch, then.

Rod's hand slid to his side and out of the cunning pocket came the cosh.

It was a beautiful little weapon, fashioned of closely woven net round a hard flexible core made with infinite care out of hundreds of scraps of tinfoil and silver paper. It had a throng to go round the wrist and a grip of smooth leather.

The watchman reached the last step and paused, regurgitated heavily, and opened the door.

Rod hit him.

It was a clumsy blow, for he was standing awkwardly, and the edge of the door had made sighting difficult. But it was heavy enough to be effective. The torch fell to the floor but did not go out. The man gave a grunt as though all breath had been driven from his body, and folded forward on to his knees.

Rod took a step back and a careful aim at the bowed

4

neck. The deliberation with which he did this was delicious.

He hit again.

Then he bent down and reached to switch off the torch beside the figure, now still. As he did so he heard a quick patter of steps and most unexpectedly a little white dog came into view. It was a terrier, as old, and almost as asthmatic as its master. Plainly both puzzled and alarmed.

Rod was as completely at a loss as he had been master of the situation a moment before.

"Good dog—there's a good old boy."

The dog drew back his upper lip in the beginnings of a snarl as Rod stepped towards him.

Gunner materialised.

"Cosh him before he barks—the ruddy little perisher."

Rod hesitated.

The whole thing was unexpected.

He hated the idea of hitting the dog, and hated himself for hesitating.

The dog whined and then growled softly, pulling with his teeth at the old man's coat sleeve.

"Crissake," said Gunner, "give me the——stick."

Rod could feel that he didn't fancy the job either: he held out the cosh.

At that moment the dog chose to seal his fate by barking. Gunner hit the dog inexpertly: first much too softly, and then from inexperience, a great deal too hard, breaking the skull.

Rod felt sick—then, with a tardy return of toughness, wiped the cosh on the coat of the still silent watchman.

He made a careful job of it, finishing off with his handkerchief.

Gunner was already busy at the safe.

Both man and boy wore canvas containers slung by

straps from their shoulders, sort of light ammunition pouches, worn over the shirt and under the waistcoat. Into them went the contents of the safe. These were considerable.

Diamond rings, signet rings, white metal watches. A little diamond bracelet watch, gold watches. There was a drawer full of old gold pieces and two or three dozen loose stones. The last drawer in the safe was locked and they guessed that it had cash in it. Probably the key was on the owner's ring in his pocket. People did things like that—left the safe key in a desk and then, with asinine carefulness, carried off the key of one of the drawers.

Whilst Gunner tried to wedge it open Rod went back once more to look at the watchman.

"Spark out," he reported, when he came back.

Gunner was plainly making no impression on the little steel drawer. He had neither the room to develop his strength on it nor the skill to pick the tiny lock.

Outside in New Oxford Street an early morning car came slowly past, seemed for a moment to be slowing down: Rod's heart thumped: at the last moment the driver accelerated and passed on.

Both of them felt it was time to be off.

Five minutes later they were standing in the back courtyard, dusting from knees and elbows the marks of the slither from the outhouse roof.

Upstairs the watchman groaned, sat up, was sick, saw the dog and began to swear.

• 2 •

Stumpi was a "White" Russian. Or rather, was thought by the Boys to be "white" on the grounds that had he been "red" he would have been chasing the rackets in his native Moscow and not in London. He kept a tiny all-night restaurant called "The Bandbox", situated in the street which bounds the northern hinterland of Leicester Square and is blanked off on one side by the backs of the big cinemas. Little was known about him except that he kept three mistresses, all in the West Central post district. ("It saves travelling," he used to say. "I am too old to voyage.")

Thither Rod and the Gunner came, at a cautious hundred yards interval. The clock at the corner of the Charing Cross Road showed half-past four and morning was not far away.

In the steamy little Bandbox there was only one customer. A rat-like person who looked up incuriously as the Gunner came in—with growing interest when Rod followed and sat down at the same table. After that first quick glance he never looked at them directly again and five minutes later he paid his bill and shuffled out.

• 3 •

In the duty room at the Yark the Junior Inspector hung up the receiver and lifted his head as Hazlerigg came in.

"Another job, sir—New Oxford Street."

"Shop?"

"Small jewellers—they coshed the watchman, but he wasn't out long. We've just had him on the phone. I've sent the patrol car. There should be something soon."

"Three in one night," said Hazlerigg. "All jewellers." The bell went again. Hazlerigg picked up the extension. "Sergeant Martin, sir. 66 New Oxford Street. I'm speaking from the caretaker's room. I've got the caretaker here. One thing might be helpful. He tells me he always went round the offices at twenty to four sharp. He was knocked out as he got to the top landing."

The Junior Inspector was looking at his log sheet and

7

interrupted: "We got his message at five to four."

"Just so, sir. He can't have been out more than ten minutes or thereabouts—must have come round just as they were going. They got out of a passage window, judging from the marks they left. There's a small court-yard there. The door's open."

"Any lead as to which way they went?"

"Not that I can see, sir. The door opens on to a pas-sage."

"Ask him," said Hazlerigg, "if there were any signs of a car having stood in the passage way."

The Junior Inspector put this question and it was ob-vious from the silence with which it was received that Sergeant Martin didn't know.

"He's going to look now," said the Inspector. "He's a good chap. Lots would have chanced it and said 'No'."

A constable brought in two cups and they were sip-ping the hot dark tea gratefully when the bell went again.

"X Division," said the Inspector. "This does sound interesting. Yes. Go on."

The Inspector reached out as he was listening and pressed a button. A red light came up on the panel. "Two cars with full crews," he said, "and warn three and four." The light blinked and went out. "Are you going, sir?"

"You bet," said Hazlerigg. "That was Stiffy, wasn't it?"

"Yes, sir—saw them five minutes ago, just by chance, coming into Stumpi's joint."

"God bless all narks," said Hazlerigg as he took the steps at a run.

• 4 •

Gunner and Rod had finished an early breakfast of sau-sages and chips served by the taciturn Stumpi, and were

8

sitting over their second cup of coffee.

Gunner was almost asleep. Rod, on the other hand, felt both fresh and alert. He possessed that quality, rare in a man and almost unknown in a boy, of being able to "back pedal" in moments of danger and stress, and this gave him the advantage of being able to coast quietly through the reactionary period that followed. It is a quality which distinguishes the greatest generals.

Where Gunner had been talkative and excited, he had been taciturn almost to the point of rudeness. And now that Gunner nodded—he was doing some thinking.

In particular he was thinking about the second part of the instructions he had had from the Chief the night before. They were all right as far as they went, but they didn't seem to Rod to go quite far enough. It had been impressed on them that they must keep away from the meeting-place until a respectable hour in the morning —"say ten o'clock," the Chief had said. "Get yourself something to eat and then have a wash and brush up. Don't go home—and don't wander about the streets unnecessarily."

Well, that was fair enough. Only mugs wandered about the streets in the small hours; it was asking to be picked up by a nosey slop looking for promotion. But it left a lot of time to kill. Then again, Stumpi might be O.K.—the boys said he was—and again he might not. He sat blinking at them from behind the corner table, apparently unwearied by his all-night session.

On an impulse Rod got to his feet and asked: "Where's the Gents?" Stumpi nodded at a curtained recess at the back. Rod found the filthy little water closet, and found something more. A door, leading out to a pint-sized area with an iron staircase. The door was bolted. Rod unbolted it. He made his way back to the shop and as he put his hand up to pull the curtain aside

9

a great many things seemed to happen at once.

The first thing his eye caught, through the steamy front window, was the bonnet of a large black car, coasting to a standstill. Then the shot front seemed to irrupt as huge figures tumbled through the door. He saw Gunner on his feet swinging a chair and the crash of splintering wood was in his ears as he made the back door. A second later he was in the area and up the steps. A quick look showed him the street was empty.

Fast as his young legs carried him, a more elderly pair of legs was moving faster still. Hazlerigg had grasped the fact that one of his birds had flown and was round in his tracks and out of the door before Gunner had finished swinging his first chair.

Without stopping to open the door of the car he pushed his head and shoulders through the side window and seized the radio head-set. "Hullo Three, hullo Four. Close on Cambridge Circus. Move fast." The set crackled. "Hullo Three—move from Cambridge Circus down Shaftesbury Avenue—watch your left. Hullo Four—move from Cambridge Circus down Charing Cross Road. Watch your right. Look out for a youth: medium height, wearing no hat or coat. That is all. Acknowledge."

As a result of these energetic measures, when Rod paused at the corner of Gerrard Street, he saved himself, for the second time, only by the quickness of his wits. He saw the police car a fraction of a second before it could have seen him, and turned on his tracks. Two minutes later he peered cautiously out of Newport Passage and realised the nature of the trap which was holding him.

His mind was still working. He had noticed, at the top end of Newport Passage, a row of tenement flats with a communal basement passage. Down into this he climbed. Stooping in the shadows he loosened the

10

buckle under his coat and wriggled clear of the heavy satchel. Quietly he picked off the top of the nearest of the many dustbins and dropped it in. As quietly he put the lid back.

Then on hands and knees he crawled for the full length of the passage. There was a door at the end. It opened to his touch.

He found himself in a sort of connecting subway which ran under the tenement from Newport Passage to the fronting street. It was pitch dark and from its smell contained a further selection of refuse bins. But the sweetest-smelling haven could not have been more welcome.

The door had a bolt and he shot it gently, before moving cautiously forward among the empty milk bottles. The door at the other end, he found, was already locked. He sat down to wait.

• 5 •

An hour later Hazlerigg called off his cordon. Half an hour after it had gone Rod slipped out. He had no means of knowing whether the way was clear or not, but an irrational feeling possessed him that his luck would hold. He recovered the satchel and disappeared circumspectly in the general direction of Seven Dials.

2

"W's the Warrior,
Home from the Wars"

Major Angus McCann was sitting in the padded splendour of a celebrated West End Hotel. He was in a mood of roaring Bolshevism which far exceeded anything under the mere general heading of being "browned off". Such a description was infinitely too tame and neutral.

It was the evening of his second day in England.

Behind him lay six completed years of soldiering in the Commandos. He had spent a colourful fortnight in Norway in early 1940, and had sniffed at unguarded portions of the coast of France. He had gone out to North Africa in 1942 and later had dropped into the sea off the coast of Sicily and had lived to bless his peacetime love of long-distance swimming. At the end of 1943 he had returned to England and spent a glorious six months assaulting, in working hours, the larger landed estates in the South Midlands—(this was known as "intensive training")—and wrecking many of the stately homes of England in a series of stupendous guest-nights. Finally, one day in early June of 1944, he had landed in Normandy and had marched to that celebrated bridge "where, to the sound of the pipes, the green berets and the red berets had met and intermingled."

The familiar spirit which had preserved his skin in these fantastic episodes was now to be worked overtime, and had stepped in with a judicious bout of jaundice, severe enough to keep him out of the area of the Arnhem salient altogether. After that things had gone smoothly enough and he had been in no real danger until the week following the Armistice when he had tried to argue with a drunken Russian soldier in one of Berlin's border-line restaurants.

Fortunately his ability to get under a table had exceeded the Russian's ability to find his automatic pistol, and all had been smoothed over.

He ordered another glass of beer and tried to look happy when asked to pay two shillings for it.

Farther along the bar he observed two girls who appeared to be taking a great deal of time over their first drinks, and he entertained the unworthy suspicion that they were waiting for a good samaritan to come and stand them the next one.

"Let 'em wait," said Major McCann ungallantly (actually they were school teachers from Saffron-Walden engaged in seeing the night life of London. The blonde one taught geography and the brunette took physical training. They drank their pink gins slowly because they disliked the taste of them. They will not appear again in this story).

Major McCann imbibed some more beer. He was honest enough to realise that he himself was very largely to blame for his own feelings. He had little of substance to complain about. He was sound in wind and limb. He had somewhere to live. He had a little money.

He shared a flat with a very much elder sister, in the wilds of North Hampstead. She was an excellent cook and a thoroughly good "manager". His bed was so soft and the sheets so exquisitely aired and laundered that he had scarcely slept a wink on his first night at home.

13

True, she was not a sparkling conversationalist and it would have been a stretch of the imagination to have described her as a kindred spirit, her main interests being afternoon bridge and British Israel.

She had displayed an altogether unexpected interest in her brother's activities in Egypt and he had been agreeably surprised thereat until it transpired that her sustaining hope had been that he might have secured some accurate measurements of the great pyramid. (They were, he gathered, connected in a vague but important way with the future of the United Nations and the development of atomic energy.)

Again he reminded himself with great fairness that it was unreasonable to be angry with anyone for being themselves and not someone else altogether. She had many excellent qualities, had survived the bombing and rocketing without stirring an inch from her appointed way of life, had undergone undoubted hardships, and had, by her own unaided efforts, saved two and a half tons of waste paper. There must be many worse people in London. Indeed, at that moment two of them came in. Major McCann felt his hackles rise as he viewed the newcomers, a man and a woman.

The man, he felt sure, was a stockbroker, and equally he felt sure that he was known to his friends as "The Major" (1914–18 vintage). His considerable body was too tightly encased in a suit which contrived to out-savile Savile Row and his startlingly pig-like face appeared at first sight to be a healthy brick-red; it was only on closer inspection that it became evident that this colour was produced by numberless little scarlet threads, the finger-prints left by high living and much old brandy. He was wearing the tie of a very well-known cricket club. His companion was a lacquered job, very partially dressed in that shade of jet satin best calculated to set off a dead white skin (or alternatively, thought McCann,

14

the dead white skin had been superimposed as best calculated to show off the jet satin—in those days of coupons it was difficult to tell where art ended and
economy began).

They were so perfectly suited to each other and to
their present surroundings that it would have caused
him no surprise had they headed a male and female
chorus respectively, and started some song and dance
ensemble.

Fitted to each other in one way, certainly. In others,
he was not so sure. He fancied the man was more likely
to get his fun out of warm and grubby little typists. And
the woman? Well, as far as she looked human at all, he
associated her with something Middle-Eastern.

He pictured her in bed with a certain Egyptian of his
acquaintance, shuddered, and finished his beer.

Quite suddenly he felt that he had had enough. The
whole place, its atmosphere, its decoration scheme, its
sleek waiters and impossible clientele, took him by the
throat. He seized his hat, disregarded the insinuating
palm of the cloakroom attendant (whose worried expression was probably due to the fact that he was having
difficulty with his surtax returns) and pushed out into
the night.

Descending Hay Hill an American soldier stopped
him.

"Mister, what time do you make it?"

"Ten past nine," said McCann. Unlike some of his
countrymen, he liked American soldiers. He had seen
them fight.

"Ten after nine, eh?"

"That's right."

"You wouldn't, perhaps, be a minute or two fast?"

McCann considered the matter.

"Well, yes, I might be," he admitted.

The American produced two heavy, expensive-looking platinum timepieces and scrutinised them carefully.

"Coming up for nine minutes past nine right now," he said. "Five—four—three—two—one—Now."

"Thank you so much. Good night."

"It's a pleasure," said the American sombrely, and rolled on his way.

Major McCann pushed on in the general direction of Shepherd's Market.

He wanted to find a pub as different as possible from the hotel he had just left. From his pre-war recollections, this was a promising area to start in.

A name came into his head. "The Pink Elephant."

"I beg your pardon," said a small man, who seemed to have materialised from the pavement.

"I'm very sorry—I was talking to myself."

"Did I hear you mention 'The Pink Elephant'?"

"That's right—a public house: somewhere in these parts, unless it's been blitzed."

"It hasn't been blitzed," said the small man. "It's been closed."

"Closed? Who by?"

"The police."

"Oh—ah—yes. I see." Thinking it over he was not really surprised. "Perhaps," he went on, "you could tell me the name of some other place."

"Depends what you want," said the small man.

"Beer—and peace and quiet."

"Try the Leopard. First right, down the steps, right again, and on your right."

"Right," said the Major. "I mean, thank you very much. I will."

"Don't mention it," said the small man, and dematerialised.

As Major McCann, following these directions, approached his objective, so a sense of familiarity grew. And when he got there he recognised it quite easily,

16

although it was (Good God!) over ten years since he had been there. The faded signboard was the same, and he remembered the three awkward steps up to the saloon bar with the metal boot scraper at the bottom. He recollected vividly falling down the one on to the other, one frosty moonless night.

He wondered if Pop still owned the place.

Pop Carter had been quite a celebrity in those far-off pre-war days. A man of middle height, thick build and indeterminate class. All things to all men. Hear him talking to the famous authors who came almost nightly to the public bar and you suspected him of having a broad and catholic imagination—listen to him swapping stories with the commercials and you were sure of it. He had acted as his own chucker-out and had been an expert practitioner with the blackthorn truncheon which hung under the serving ledge. Had he not laid out with it "Rufus" Gavigan the very night that enterprising gentleman had finished attending to the London office of the Société Anonyme, and had come to celebrate his million franc haul on Pop's Four Star, with the result that whilst policemen beat through the streets and restaurants, bars and brothels of the West End, Rufus lay happily unconscious in the casualty ward of the Middlesex Hospital.

"Where's Mr. Carter?" he asked the woman behind the bar.

"He's dead," said the woman. "Been dead for five years."

"I'm sorry to hear that. I knew him well in the old days. Perhaps you remember him yourself."

"I ought to," said the woman. "He was my father." She said it, however, without malice.

The Major really looked at her for the first time. He remembered, now, that Pop had possessed a wife, who sometimes "obliged" in the saloon bar, and a family

17

who had never made a public appearance at all. He had heard that there was a daughter who had gone to a school "above her station". This was probably the one. She seemed pleasant and capable.

"Have something yourself," he suggested.

She gave him a quick look and paid him the compliment of accepting a gin and lime.

"I remember your father," he said, "a very remarkable man. Quite outstanding in his own line."

"He was a dear," said Miss Carter, with unexpected warmth. "You heard what happened to him?"

"No—I've been out of touch lately."

"He and Mother together—it happened about the end of the first blitz. Were you in England then?"

"Yes," said the Major, "but not in London, thank Heaven."

"I never knew two people who took less notice of things like that. You know—bombs and noises. I used to be scared stiff. And when a big one came especially near I'd start downstairs for the shelter. Then I'd stop for a minute and listen at their door. And I'd hear them snoring. So I'd hop back into bed. Pride's a funny thing."

"So's breeding," thought the Major. "It sticks out a mile, wherever you find it."

He was often surprised at the frequency with which perfect strangers confided their life histories to him. Only that morning a man from whom he had stopped to buy a newspaper at the corner of Panton Street had spent a quarter of an hour taking him through the details of a rather optimistic pension claim.

Miss Carter returned from serving a customer with whisky (of which she seemed to have an almost pre-war stock) and picked up her gin and lime and the thread of her story.

"After all," she said, "the house never lost so much as

18

a pane of glass. Mother and Father were killed walking down Regent Street. It was the last bomb of the last bad raid we had in the West End."

She stared dreamily into the cloudy centre of her glass and the Major wondered what she was seeing in it. Metal, flame, smoke, destruction, mutilation. Cordite blackened clothes. Grey skin and the rich plum colour of newly shed blood.

Or nothing at all.

"Don't talk about it if it worries you," he said.

"It used to worry me," said Miss Carter. "Oh dear, how it used to worry me. But hard work's a good cure for worry. The old man owned this place—freehold, goodwill and all. It's not a brewer's house, you know. And not a penny out on mortgage. I've been running it ever since. Coming, sir—same again?"

It couldn't be an easy place to run. The Leopard was not only a pub, it was a "Residential" as well. That is to say, it had half a dozen rooms available for bed and breakfast. If Pop Carter had liked you, you might stay there any time from six days to six months, a pleasant, rather hand-to-mouth existence which entailed taking your midday meal out and sharing the evening meal with the family. If Pop Carter had disliked you, your stay would have been more in the neighbourhood of six minutes, or even six seconds.

"I've got plenty of rooms," he once said to a stout business man who appeared to be travelling with his secretary—(possibly pressure of work dictated his idea that they should share the same bedroom)—"but you're not having one. And you can sue me for refusing to take you in. And if you do I shall charge you with stealing one of my silver tankards from the private bar. I lost three last week."

Not that there had been much logic in the old man's choices. It was just a question of like and dislike. He

19

remembered "Glasgow". She had been one of his oldest tenants. What had happened to her, he wondered.

Miss Carter anticipated the question by remarking as she returned: "If you knew Pop well, you probably met Miss Macduff."

"I certainly did," said the Major.

"She's still with us—the last of the old faithfuls. Perhaps you'd like to run up and have a word with her. She moved up to Number Ten during the blitz. Said the nearer she got to heaven the better. Do run up. She'd love to see you."

The Major climbed the stairs and knocked at No. 10.

"Come away in," said the well-remembered voice.

Glasgow was sitting on the edge of her bed, comfortably if informally dressed in a polo-necked primrose sweater and a kimono; and, as the Major became increasingly aware, very little else. She raised at him the bland appraising look which had first set his heart beating to double time ten years and more since.

"Why, Angus—you're a sight for sore eyes. Sit down and talk to an old woman."

She cleared a space for him on the bed by sweeping a few of the things that were there already off on to the floor.

"London's a cold sad place, these days. It's only old friends that keep me from drink and worse."

"What's worse than drink, Glasgow?" he said, affectionately licking up her hand.

"Come away, come away," said Miss Macduff sternly, giving him, nevertheless, an affectionate squeeze. "No tricks, now, or I'll be obliged to scream."

"Surely you know me better than that," said the Major.

"Aye, too well. It's good to see you, though. Will you take a cup of tea? Bide awhile, and I'll put the kettle on."

She padded into the next room.

The Major had no real desire for tea on top of all the beer he had drunk, but hesitated to hurt her feelings. A compromise occurred to him.

"Leave the tea," he said. "Get some knickers on and come down and have a drink in the private bar."

Over a generous whisky Glasgow sat and listened to McCann's opinion of the inhabitants of London.

"I'm not thin skinned," he said, "but there's no getting away from it, I have got a weakness for courtesy in the ordinary dealings of life. This morning now, I jumped on to a bus which was waiting for the traffic lights. Apparently it was full up. Well, you could hardly describe that as my fault, could you? If it had happened before the war a firm but more or less polite conductor would have called my attention to the fact that I constituted one in excess of the lawful number appointed to be carried by the vehicle in question, and would have requested me to alight at the first stop. What happened to-day? A henna-haired bitch (excuse me, Glasgow, she really was a bitch) started screaming at me from the top of the stairs. Since I was unable (fortunately) to understand what she was saying, and quite unable to dismount owing to the speed at which the bus was travelling, I took no action. Whereupon she descended the stairs and delivered a sharp and unexpected blow in the middle of my chest. It was only by clinging with the tenacity of a limpet that I managed to save my footing. I suppose my correct course of action would have been to have allowed myself to fall and break a leg and then to have sued the London Passenger Transport Board. Pah!"

"All conductresses are bitches," said Glasgow soothingly. "Pray Heaven we'll soon have the boys back."

"Then the tobacconists. Do you know, I'm already afraid to ask for a packet of cigarettes. You'd hardly think that such a simple matter could present any difficulties. I dare say you don't even notice it? No. You've got used to it gradually. If it's a man behind the counter you take your chance. You can be snappy and business-like and adopt a sort of 'no black market here' tone of voice—or you can be man-to-man and confidential. In either case the result's the same. You get no cigarettes— or ten of a brand you don't want. If it's a girl you feel compelled to act like a dago dancing partner making advances to a hat-check girl, in the faint hope that she's got twenty Gold Flake under the counter."

"All girls in tobacconists' shops are bitches," said Glasgow. "Have this one on me."

At some period in the evening McCann had bought an evening paper and as Glasgow disappeared in quest of further whisky he pulled it out of his pocket and read on the front page:

CRIME WAVE HITS OXFORD STREET

Last night, and early this morning, two jew-ellers' shops in Oxford Street were broken into. At the first, the thieves had a poor haul since they were unable to make any impression on the firm's safe. At the other, the shop and premises of Cartwright & Gladstone, they removed articles to the value of £1,500, including watches, bracelets and loose stones. Mr. Finkelstein, the manager . . . [followed a long and unconvincing statement from Mr. Finkelstein, in which he tried, without con-spicuous success to explain away his folly in leav-ing the safe key in an unlocked drawer].

After a brutal attack on the night watchman, a Mr. Parrot, the intruders committed the wanton outrage of killing a white terrier belonging to the watchman, which had evidently tried to interfere with their nefarious activities.

22

A man has already been detained by the police in connection with the latter robbery.

It is not known whether the two affairs were connected, but certain similarities in technique suggest, etc., etc.

He retailed the story to Glasgow when she came back with the drinks. "Brutes like that deserve whipping," he said.

"Aye—they do that," agreed Glasgow. "Poor little dog."

"Poor little watchman."

"He's paid to take risks," said Glasgow. "Dogs are different. Poor dumb creature. People aren't going to like that."

She was right, of course.

The great British public would watch unmoved the despoliation of a hundred merchant jewellers and the stunning, binding, gagging and maltreating of their servants. But to hurt a dog or a child—that was unspeakable. Chief Inspector Hazlerigg knew this, too, and it was at his insistence that the newspapers had plugged the story.

"Just one more then, dearie," agreed Glasgow.

The evening was attaining an alcoholic momentum of its own, and since good things never come singly the Major did not feel surprised when the door opened and Sergeant Dalgetty walked in.

When Glasgow saw the green beret she proffered her farewells and departed upstairs like the good, kind, tactful creature she was. She had lived by her wits for nearly half a century and knew when to leave a party. A priceless knowledge, which was lacking in many of her betters. Sergeant Dalgetty had not only been in McCann's Company, but he was a very old and very tried friend. In the early days of the war the Major, then a subaltern, had steered the Sergeant through the exceedingly tricky consequences of a week-end's absence without leave (taken to settle a matrimonial difference); and in Norway the Sergeant had saved McCann's life. Even this had failed to terminate their friendship.

As the air grew thick with smoke and the long hand crept towards closing time, so was the past relived. Every sentence seemed to begin with "Do you remember——?" and the old magical names floated to the surface and burst into a froth of reminiscence. Stavanger and Vasterival, Bone and Sedgenane, Le Port and Wesel. "Do you remember Nobby and Blanco trying to load a Jerry Eighty-eight with a twenty-five pounder shell?" said Sergeant Dalgetty. "'Won't go in,' Nobby said, 'hit the——with a mallet. Anything'll go in if you hit it hard enough.' No, come to think of it, that was when you were in hospital."

"Time, gentlemen, please," said the barmaid.

"And that time we tried what would happen if we fired a nine-inch mortar straight up in the air. . . ."

"Time, gentlemen, *please*."

As they stood on the pavement for a moment, the Sergeant said: "Talking of Blanco, I saw him last week —at the corner of Berkeley Square and Davies Street, about seven o'clock. I gave him a shout, but he can't have heard me. Funny thing, just dived into the doorway. A block of offices."

"I can't quite see Blanco as a black-coated worker," said the Major. "One of our rougher diamonds. Good night, Sergeant. I've got your address, good. We'll be seeing some more of each other before long. Good night."

It was a lovely night. There was a half moon up, and a light wind packing the clouds across. The Major thought he would walk. He plunged into the well-ordered patchwork of by-ways which lies between Piccadilly and Oxford Street. He was scarcely troubling to steer a course since he was well aware that Park Lane on the left or Regent Street on the right would prevent him from tacking too far. In consequence he found it difficult, when thinking it over afterwards, to fix his exact whereabouts at the moment when he became conscious of footsteps running behind him.

There is always a temptation to observe without being observed. He drew back into the shadow of a convenient doorway. The steps came nearer.

Without being able to define his reasons precisely, the Major felt interested. The runner was so clearly afraid of being followed and anxious to evade whoever might be following him. Every fifty yards he would stop for an instant to collect his breath and listen, then on again. He was wearing rubber soled shoes, too.

As the play of the moonlight fitfully lit up the empty road the man drew nearer.

Now it must be emphasised that the Major was not at the time absolutely and strictly sober. Far, far from drunk—(even in the military sense of that difficult word). But it was undeniable that he had placed a number of whiskies and brandies on top of a pint or so of beer. And, as many a drinker had found to his cost, had committed the additional indiscretion of placing further pints on top of the whisky.

The fact remains, excuse it how you will, that as the runner drew level with Major McCann, the latter became a victim of an uncontrollable impulse.

He thrust his leg out.

The results exceeded expectations, and the runner, his momentum being checked at the base, whilst his upper parts persisted in their forward progress, described a graceful half-circle.

The Major jumped forward.

Even in the stress of the moment he noticed the skill

and precision with which the unknown regained his footing. It was a skill born of the gymnasium and the boxing ring—a precision of the cheap *palais de danse*.

The Major, wondering for the moment whether he was arresting a malefactor or assisting the victim of an accident, laid hold of the man's coat.

A white weasel face looked up at him.

There was a barely perceptible movement, the slurring sound of the parting of rotten cloth, and the Major was standing once more alone in the moonlit road.

In his hand he held the remains of a jacket pocket.

A black saloon car slid up. A gleam of silver along the roof showed the tell-tale wireless mast.

"Excuse me," said an offensively polite voice, "but perhaps you can assist us. We are looking for a youth in connection with a burglary. . . ."

"Aye," said the Major. "A young keelie."

"I beg your pardon."

"A young hooligan. I heard him running and tried to stop him. Here's some of his jacket."

"Thank you," said the voice gravely. "Straight ahead?"

"Aye, straight ahead."

The car shot on.

The excitements of the night were not yet quite over. When McCann got back to his Hampstead flat he found a note from his sister propped against the clock.

"Inspector Hazlerigg rang up this evening. He will ring you again to-morrow."

3

The Strings of a Racket

"I expect," said Inspector Hazlerigg, "that you find London a bit noisy after the peacefulness of occupied Germany."

"Quite so," agreed Major McCann shortly. He was not feeling at his happiest, nor was he a man who disguised his feelings easily. "I've been in Austria, not Germany," he added.

"A charming country. The Tyrol especially, and Carinthia. It always seemed to me to combine the best of Germany and the best of Switzerland."

"No doubt," said the Major. "I was in Vienna."

In addition to a very healthy hang-over—not so much the result of excess as of a too cordial mingling of the grain and the grape—he was suffering from that slight feeling of wariness which comes over even the most law-abiding the first time they make contact with the police machine.

Absurd, of course.

Hazlerigg seemed anxious to put his visitor's mind at rest. "I am sorry to drag you down here so soon after your return," he went on, "but what I have to ask you is highly confidential and even slightly irregular—it is emphatically not the sort of thing which could have been said over the telephone. Have a cigarette? They are part of the office props. I don't have to pay for them."

McCann accepted a cigarette and relaxed provisionally.

"I got your name," went on the Inspector, "from your Regimental Association. They told me you were due back this week-end, so I took a chance and rang you up—spoke to your sister." Hazlerigg hitched himself closer and leaned forward across the desk. "I expect you're wondering what it's all about."

McCann agreed.

"Well, it's like this. You may have read in the papers that we've been suffering recently from what is popularly known as a crime-wave."

"We didn't get many papers in Vienna," said McCann. "I seem to remember something about it. Has it abated yet?" he added politely.

"Not so's you'd notice it. Rather the contrary. The tide is coming in. A few days ago, on Sunday evening, or, to be precise, very early on Monday morning, two jewellers' shops in New Oxford Street were broken into. In one of them the thieves got nothing much for their pains, and made a safe, but comparatively inexpensive get-away."

"Too bad."

"In the other, however, a considerable haul of watches and jewellery was made."

"I read about it," said McCann. "Wasn't that where the swine killed the watchman's terrier?"

"That's correct—and got away with over a thousand pounds' worth of stuff."

"I hope you catch them," said McCann, "and have them flogged. You can still flog for robbery with violence, can't you?"

"We have caught them," said Hazlerigg, "or rather,

28

we've caught one of them. We got him red-handed, a few hours after the burglary, with half the stuff on him. I think you know him. His name is Andrews—John Patrick Andrews, known to his friends as 'Gunner'. He was in your company, I understand."

To say that McCann was surprised would be an understatement.

"Andrews! We certainly had an Andrews. He came to us from one of the Artillery Regiments, and now that you mention it, I believe he was called 'Gunner' by his friends. But he was a decent lad—it's difficult to think of him as a criminal."

"I thought that he seemed a reasonable type of man," agreed Hazlerigg. "For instance, he carried no weapon of any sort. Not even a stick. And he was certainly a fighter. When we took him in an all-night café he broke two chairs and a table on my men before they could get him down. We don't mind that sort of thing, you know. It makes the men feel they're earning their pay."

"But Andrews, a crook," said McCann. "I'd have gone bail that he was straight. Look here, Inspector, I suppose you're absolutely certain . . ."

"Red-handed—he hasn't even bothered to deny it."

"One thing, if he *is* a criminal, and I suppose I'll have to take your word for it, he hasn't lost any time, has he?"

Hazlerigg made an indeterminate noise which McCann interpreted as agreement.

"I mean to say—he's only been demobbed about three months. Possibly less. And I shouldn't have said that he was naturally that way inclined. He didn't come from the gutter."

The Inspector said: "I've asked you down here to help us, and if you're going to help us it's only fair that you should know something of what this is all about. I can't fill in the details myself, but I can give you an outline. I need hardly tell you that this is confidential. Top secret, I believe that's the correct term. Very well then——"

Hazlerigg talked easily and well. And as he talked Major McCann had the impression that a light was going up in a quarter of which he had hitherto known very little. He had the ordinary newspaper reader's knowledge of the great daily battle between organised wrong and organised right. And it began to dawn on him that he had known as little about it, really, as the man in the street had known about the realities of this war.

Less.

For in war there is a certain morale-building value in the work of a good war correspondent which has led to the toleration of accurate front-line reporting. Whilst in the war against crime, the veil is only rarely and briefly lifted.

The results are shown all right with all the intermediate steps left out.

"The police are seeking a Mr. Albert Brown of Putney for questioning in connection with the recent demise of Mr. Sidney White: Mr. White, it will be remembered, was found early yesterday morning with serious head wounds. . . ."

"Before the war," Hazlerigg said, "it wasn't so bad. In modern jargon, we had 'parity of forces'. But just at this moment I can't disguise from you things aren't so good. Some of the reasons are temporary ones—we had them after the last war—like the shortage of trained men, illegal firearms, the presence of foreign deserters, and so on. Time will cure them quickly enough, I've no doubt. But there's something else, too."

His heavy, Cromwellian face looked so serious that McCann was genuinely startled.

"We're up against something altogether new in crime —new, that is, so far as this country is concerned. It is something like what the Americans call a 'racket'—but a racket with some odd strings in it. Here's what's happened so far. Early this spring we started getting a large number of house breakings and shop burglaries, all carrying the same trade mark. I don't mean that the guilty party signed his name in chalk on the safe door, or any boy-scoutery of that sort. But there were signs, enough in the end to add up to a certainty that the jobs were being planned by the same group of people. Planned, you see, not executed. You had technical courses in the army, didn't you?"

"We certainly did," said McCann.

"Well then, if you were watching a bunch of recruits doing their musketry, or mine lifting, or signalling, I expect you'd soon pick out the man who had been on a course. A lot of little details would show that he had been professionally coached—particularly if the coaching was recent."

"Good God," said McCann. "What an extraordinary idea. Are you telling me that someone has been running a nursery for criminals?"

"It looks like it," said Hazlerigg, with no answering smile. "In fact, once you accept the inherent improbability, it sticks out a mile. The way the back windows are always opened, the technique for dealing with bolted doors, the fact that a night-watchman who interferes is always coshed—and in the same way—while a householder who comes on the scene is terrorised and tied up. The proper use of sticking plaster as a gag—even the knots in the silk stockings with which the lady of the house is tied to her own bed."

"But what makes you think that this is the result of a crime-school? All the jobs you are talking about might have been done by the same man."

"I can give you two good reasons," said Hazlerigg grimly. "The first is that we're getting from ten to twenty

31

of these jobs *every month*. The second is that we've already caught several of the actual executives. Apart from Andrews, whom we pulled in last night, we've got our hands on seven of the people who were actually responsible for the burglaries. Now see what you make of this. In every case it was their first or second job. None of them had a shred of criminal record. Four of them were boys between the ages of fourteen and seventeen. The other three were young men just out of the army—in two cases deserters. In the other case, a man who had been recently demobbed.

Both men were silent for a moment and some of the implications of what had been said came home to the soldier. He shifted uneasily in his chair and looked out at the sunlight and the white gulls scavenging on Waterloo Embankment. It was McCann who broke the silence.

"I see," he said; "not pretty."

"I wonder if you realise quite how dangerous and damnable it is," said the other. "We're up against a perverted psychologist. He's using the most explosive material—the natural lawlessness of these kids and the restless dissatisfaction of the demobbed soldier."

"And I suppose they'll none of them talk——"

"Of course not. You know what kids are on loyalty and not telling tales."

"And we've been six years inculcating the same thing into a lot of grown-up children," agreed McCann, "under the name of *esprit de corps*."

"Even if they did talk," said Hazlerigg, "I doubt if they could tell us much. But there's something else which is shutting their mouths. The most powerful gag in the world. Plain fear.

"Quite early on in the proceedings we had a stroke of luck. Or it seemed so at the time. One of our sergeants —a very promising lad, called Pollock—had got himself into the army. I don't know how he did it, but he was accepted for the infantry in August 1939—breaking about half a dozen rules to get there. He had a good war until he stopped a shell splinter in his knee on the Sangro crossing. He came home on indefinite sick-leave and in early 1944 we had him seconded to our plainclothes branch to help the Security people. This job took him into some pretty odd places, and he found his best 'cover' was to pose as a deserter from his old mob. It was easy for him—he had the jargon right and it was a long-odds chance against meeting anyone who would recognise him as an officer. He did some damned sound work—we were very busy, as you know, at that time starting the cover plan for the Normandy business.

"Last November he came along with an odd story. A friend of his (who really *was* a deserter, by the way) had asked him if he'd like to make some 'real money'. The idea appeared to be that he should try his hand at house-breaking. This was a normal enough proposition, in the circles he was moving in just then, but what *was* odd was the degree of organisation and preparation in the mob who were apparently financing the job. Amongst other interesting items he was told that he would be 'insured'. That is to say, that should he be pinched, due to bad luck rather than his own stupidity, the sum of £200 would be paid to any dependent or nominee he cared to appoint. The idea tickled him so much that he accepted at once—and came round to tell me all about it.

"He then went to keep a final appointment with his 'contact'. Three days later the Deptford police found Pollock's body in the cellar of a blitzed house. The rats had been at him for about forty-eight hours. But the worst damage had quite clearly taken place before death. You're probably hardened to beastliness, but I don't think I'll tell you what actually had been done to him. However, someone had clearly had a good deal of fun over killing him, and they had taken their time over it. Next day I got an envelope. It was addressed to me personally, office number and all. It had £200 in it."

McCann said: "Let me see that I have got the facts quite clear, Inspector. You are telling me that a body of men is engaged in large-scale organised robbery. They are using boys and recently demobilised soldiers to do the actual work. These operatives, if they are caught, either won't or can't or daren't tell you anything about the central organisation."

"Correct. Now, I can tell you a little more than that. The only things which are stolen are gold, silver and stones—sometimes gold and silver watches, and loose cash. Another thing—and this is perhaps the most extraordinary thing of all. Although every article stolen has been carefully circularised and full descriptions have appeared in the *Police Gazette* and *Pawn Brokers' List*, we haven't been able to trace a single item, stone or bracelet or watch."

"There may be a very simple explanation of that," suggested McCann. "Perhaps they haven't sold any of them yet."

"Maybe," said Hazlerigg. "If so, where's the money coming from? An organisation like this one isn't run on charity and bad cheques."

"Then perhaps the goods have been disposed of abroad. Of course you'll have considered all these points long ago. I'm just thinking aloud."

"Carry on," said Hazlerigg. "It's helpful. Funny you should mention the idea of selling the stuff abroad, because I think there *is* a foreign angle to it. But it's not very easy to figure it out. About six months ago we had our eyes on a man who might easily have been connected with this mob. There wasn't anything very definite on him. His name was 'Beany' Cole and he was a

34

small-time yeg and 'elastic' man of the sort that are sixpence the dozen on Frith Street and Greek Street. The
only remarkable thing about him was that he was definitely in the cash. Quite unexpectedly so."

"Possibly a legacy from a rich aunt."

"Possibly," agreed Hazlerigg. "Well, one fine morning
Beany blew into a jeweller's shop in Bond Street and
produced out of his pocket three perfect rubies in a
brooch setting. The jeweller nearly jumped out of his
frock coat. He knew they were real—and he knew
Beany.

"'I want you to price these for me,' says Beany, without batting an eyelid. 'And if you're interested, why, you
shall have first offer, Mr. Rosenbaum. I'm always
pleased to do a friend a good turn.'

"'Certainly, certainly, says Rosenbaum, 'I'll do it right
now. Would you like to wait?' and he dives into his back
office and does some telephoning; also incidentally
makes a second and closer examination of the rubies,
which really were beauties.

"Well, I won't bore you with the details of what transpired, except that we put our official foot into it good
and proper, and eventually had to apologise to Beany
and withdraw with what dignity was left to us. For, surprising as it may seem, that brooch had *not* been stolen.
It's provenance was almost unnaturally clear. It belonged to the Contessa Prebendini di Alto-Cavallo.
Beany had a letter saying so, and a telegram to our people in Rome settled the matter; moreover no question of
smuggling arose. The jewels had been in England since
before the war and were part of a collection which the
Contessa was realising in an effort to raise some funds in
England. Most of the stuff came on to the market in the
next few weeks."

"Did Beany explain why the Contessa had chosen
him? Surely there must have been dozens of reputable

jewellers or agents who would have done the job much better."

"Yes, he even explained that. He said, quite truly, that it was possible to get a lot more by a quiet and gradual realisation than by a lump sale in the auction or open market. The Contessa had got on to him through an army friend in Italy. He had been chosen because he knew the jewellers."

"Perhaps he was telling the truth."

"Perhaps he was. The last part of his statement was true enough. He does know the jewellers. If I'm not very much mistaken he was driving the car when the boys knocked off the Asiatic Diamond Company's showcase in broad daylight last week, and ran down the policeman who tried to stop them. But we haven't succeeded in proving it yet.

"We're not exactly sitting down under all this," went on Hazlerigg, "but I won't bore you with the story of our counter-measures. Most of them have been futile, and the few that haven't aren't really my secret, so I couldn't discuss them with you."

"May I speak quite plainly," said McCann. "I'm not going to ask you why you've taken me so far into your confidence, because I'm not a fool, and I can see quite plainly what you want me to do. You want me to see Andrews and try somehow to break down his natural reticence about the background of the job he's just done."

"Yes."

"You're banking on the fact that he was in my Company, and knew me well and, I thought, trusted me. In fact, you're asking for a breach of confidence. I've got to play up the role of regimental officer and father confessor and see if I can get anything out of him for your purposes?"

"It does sound rather dirty when you put it that way.

But remember, it isn't going to hurt him. If he says nothing, he goes down for this job. It's a first offence, and taking his army career and everything else into account he'll probably get off with two years."

"And if he talks?"

"I can offer no promise of any sort. But it certainly won't make it any harder for him."

"How important is all this?" asked McCann.

Hazlerigg was silent for so long that he wondered if he had offended him. At last he said: "At the moment England is living on credit. Anyone who is behind the scenes will tell you this. Indeed you don't need to be behind the scenes to know it. We're getting business from outsiders because they trust us. I don't only mean trade orders, but insurance, banking, international selection trusts, the sort of thing we've been living on for years because we represent absolute stability in a world of shifting currencies and repudiated debts. This is only a little thing so far but—the British insurance rate for movables went up ninepence in the pound this month."

"Yes," said McCann. "When you look at it like that one's own little feelings of right and decency do seem to look a bit part-worn. Thank you for being so patient with me. What do you want me to find out?"

"There are three lines to try. First of all, there must be a headquarters somewhere, and I think it's in London. To tell you the truth I'm not very hopeful about this, because I don't suppose a minor character like Andrews was ever allowed near headquarters. My guess is that they gave him a rendezvous in a pub or teashop or waiting-room and briefed him there. In fact, the Big Boys probably kept him on a string for some time until they were quite sure of him. The process may have taken months and involved half a dozen meeting-places, but I'll bet they were none of them within a mile of headquarters."

"But if we knew them we could watch them," said McCann eagerly.

If Hazlerigg noticed the change of personal pronoun, he said nothing.

"Second," he went on, "there must be at least four—perhaps half a dozen—men at the top who are really running the show. Might be women, too, I suppose, though I've never met a lady mobster yet. If Andrews ever met anyone who seemed to be a boss, or to have more authority than the others, then we'd like all the details he can give us. Last, and perhaps most important of all. Does he know of any jobs which have been planned for the future? Does he know any of the executives who are being groomed now for a forthcoming stardom?"

"Right," said McCann. "I've got all that. If you're agreeable I think I'd better see Andrews alone."

"Much better—I've had him brought along here under cover. The great thing is to keep the limelight off him. If he does talk we'll have to give him extra protection."

Later, when McCann considered the foregoing conversation in the light of subsequent knowledge, he was constrained to take his hat off to the Inspector. It seemed to him incredible that a man so overworked and hardly pressed should have had time and the patience to deal so fully and tactfully with him, to meet his objections, and to answer almost impertinent questions.

And all for so little. For such a slender hope.

Something which seemed at the time hardly worth the doing.

"Cor suffering——" said Gunner Andrews. "Here's the Major. Glad to see you, sir. How are you finding Civvy Street?"

The tone was unrepentant, but McCann, who knew his man, could sense something of what was going on behind the cockney face. He took the only other seat in the bare apartment, and said:

"I'm sorry to see you here, Andrews. What came over you?"

"Boredom, sir. Perishing boredom. Satan finds work for idle hands to do."

"What about your old job?"

"Ah," said Andrews. "Well, my old job was what you might describe as seasonal employment—very seasonal. And last October wasn't the right season."

The Major consulted the well-ordered card-index of his memory.

"You were a machine-minder."

"That's right," agreed Andrews. "That's what the book said. A machine-minder. I used to mind machines on Clinton pier. 'What the butler saw'—and that sort of thing. Well, Clinton pier's kaput—and anyway, it didn't seem to be the sort of job I fancied. Not now."

The Major had a vivid mental picture of Andrews as he had once seen him, setting out on patrol, blackened face under balaclava helmet, a belt full of German stick grenades, and a short but lethal length of iron railing in his hand.

"But how did you get into this racket?" he said, trying to keep any undue sympathy out of his voice.

"Well, sir, Curly and me——" he paused. "No offence, of course, but how much of this goes higher up?" He jerked his thumb at the ceiling.

"All of it," said the Major firmly. "Don't you see that it's the only way?"

"You a stool!" said Andrews, more in sorrow than in anger. "It doesn't hardly seem possible."

"I'll take any hard names you like if it'll make you listen to sense. For God's sake stop thinking of yourself for a minute. Think of your wife and kids."

"They're all right," said Andrews quietly.

39

Inspiration visited the Major.

"What are they getting?" he asked. "Don't tell me if you'd rather not. A hundred quid? Two hundred at the outside." He saw that the shot had gone home. "How long do you think you'll be inside for this business?"

"It's a first offence," said Andrews quickly—rather too quickly. "They say I'll get off with a year—I've got my army record—what do you think, sir?"

"I don't know who 'they' might be, but I've just heard an estimate from someone who ought to know. Two to five years. Robbery with violence."

"I never used no violence. That was that ruddy little half-pint pot with me."

"Haven't you heard of a principal in the first degree? You were there when the violence was used. That's enough to make you guilty of it. You can be flogged for violence." The brutality was not unintentional. He could see Andrews was shaken.

"Say you get off with two years," he went on. "That works out at a hundred pounds a year. That's a handsome sort of compensation for a prison record—something which will hang round your neck for the rest of your life. A hundred a year. Chicken feed! Any man with five fingers on his hands is worth at least three times that at the present moment."

"What's done's done," said Andrews sullenly.

"Certainly it's done, but that doesn't mean that we can't do anything more about it. If that was so I wouldn't be here. I'd be wasting my time somewhere else. If you'd think for a moment you'd see the police angle. They're not all that interested in you; it's the higher-ups they're after, the big league players. They aren't making any promises, but if you give them a lead up to the top, I shouldn't be surprised if somehow or other your case came to be overlooked in the general excitement. These things can be arranged, you know.

Even if that wasn't possible, you must realise that there's all the difference in the world between a short sentence of imprisonment, with the authorities on your side and everybody willing to forgive and forget, and a term of penal servitude."

Andrews grunted.

"Another thing—there's the Regimental Association. It's a poor argument, because they'll probably help you anyway. The least they can do is to keep an eye on your family. But I can really get them moving on your behalf. We'll get you a good lawyer, for a start."

McCann wondered if all this sounded as nonsensical to Andrews as it did to him. Andrews hardly seemed to be listening to him. His eyes were on the dusty sash window and his lips were moving quietly. Not hysterically, but as if he was an unpractised orator rehearsing his first speech.

McCann had the sense to keep quiet.

Andrews finally turned. A good deal of the last six years looked out of his eyes.

"By Christ, I wish I was out of this," he said. "It's good of you to try and help me, sir. And don't think I don't appreciate it. I was a mug to get into this game. It doesn't do no harm to realise you're a mug. But I can't tell you what you want to know. If I did——"

His lips kept moving silently, mumbling over a string of words. But all he said out loud was: "I suppose you think I'm being a fool, sir."

"Aye," said McCann, "I do. I think you're being every sort of bloody fool. But I also see that you've made your mind up. Well, *you* may regard the matter as settled, but I don't. I shall always be handy if you want me. And I'll do what I can for you. It probably won't be much."

Five minutes later he was trying to make sense out of this conversation for Hazlerigg's benefit.

41

"I thought for a moment that he was going to talk. It wasn't my lucid patter about legal aid. I don't think he heard me. His thoughts were on their own tack. Then, for no reason at all, he jammed. Don't ask me why, because I'm not a thought-reader. I saw from the look in his eye that he'd made his mind up. For the time being, anyway."

"Pity," said Hazlerigg. "Go back again over everything he said. Any little thing might give us a lead."

"I'm afraid that I did most of the talking. Oh, one thing. He was most emphatic that it wasn't him that coshed the watchman. He said it was the 'ruddy little half-pint pot with him'. That sounds like one of your juvenile delinquents."

"Yes, we knew there was a kid with him. Our informant told us that. Well, it's a pity, but it can't be helped. I'm sure you did your best."

The Major felt that he was being dismissed. He screwed up a considerable degree of moral courage and said rather abruptly:

"Can I help you?"

"You have helped us," said Hazlerigg courteously.

McCann ignored this.

"I'm at a loose end. I live in London, and I don't mind work." He didn't mind danger, either, but he didn't say so. If Hazlerigg hadn't gathered that from a study of his record it wasn't up to him to say as much.

"That Sergeant you lost," he went on, "Pollock—that was his name, wasn't it?—he must have been handicapped from the start by the fact that half the crooks in London knew him."

Hazlerigg hesitated. He was captivated for a moment by the sincerity of the offer. The inevitable doubts flooded in.

What would the Assistant Commissioner in charge of C.I.D. say? What would the Commissioner say? Above all, what would the public say, through its supreme mouthpiece, His Majesty's Secretary of State for Home Affairs; if something should happen to McCann.

As it certainly would.

He said rather weakly: "If a situation arises in which we could use your services, I will get in touch with you."

McCann saw that he had lost and felt an unreasonable spasm of anger against the man behind the desk and the officialdom which he represented.

He picked his hat up, ignored Hazlerigg's placatory handshake, and made his way to the door. He was just grown-up enough not to slam it.

He lost direction promptly in the maze of branching corridors, and by the time that he had inquired his way out into the open he had cooled down enough to realise that he was behaving rather stupidly.

Further, he had behaved rather naughtily. By concealing the one real tit-bit of genuine information which had come to him so fortuitously.

"Curly!"

When he had asked Andrews, point blank, how he had got into the racket, he had started, "Me and Curly..." and had then pulled himself up.

Curly was Curly White or Blanco White. The man whom Sergeant Dalgetty had told him he had seen in Berkeley Square. Curly was a very rough character indeed. And he had been a great friend of Andrews.

It was a lead.

Every particle of common sense which he possessed told him that this lead should be placed in the hands of the police. Every ounce of McCann's Scotch pride said that he was——if he would. They had turned down his proffer of help. Not exactly turned it down, perhaps, but made it quite obvious that they didn't intend to use it.

Very well.

He would follow out this private and exclusive little piece of information himself, and see where it led.

The day suddenly seemed brighter, the sun shone with a beneficial warmth and Major McCann felt happy for the first time since landing in England.

As happy as any unworldly little fly, fitting and twirling lightheartedly towards the spider's carefully camouflaged web.

He turned into Whitehall.

He was not even experienced enough to know that he was being followed.

4
Beginner's Luck

Hazlerigg studied the report which a uniformed constable had just left on his desk. As he read it he pivoted solidly in his chair and the chair squeaked in protest.

It was a monastic little office for a Chief Inspector. Curtainless windows let the light on to worn linoleum. A square "partner's" desk and a swivel chair. The only notable feature of the desk was that it had three telephones on it. One on the public line, one on the house line, one on the special line.

In the corner of the office stood a camp bed. Hazlerigg had slept there every night since Folder 26 had opened. Folder 26 was the Yard's unromantic name for the series of happenings, some of which Major McCann had just learned of.

In so far as the folder had any exact location in space it was represented by the set of filing cabinets standing behind the Inspector's desk. These were of a pattern peculiar to Scotland Yard, being small models in facsimile of the big cabinets in the basement which housed the millions of entries in the Records Department. The cards were identically slotted. So that if, for instance, one of Hazlerigg's suspects left a fingerprint behind him the card on which it was filed could be put through the selector; and in an astonishingly small number of minutes a name would be put to its owner; provided of course that the owner was a previous customer.

So far none of them had been, which didn't make life any easier. In fact, life was far from easy, just at the moment. Hazlerigg had seen the Commissioner that morning. The Commissioner had been both kind and, considering all things, appreciative. He was known as a man who backed his heads of department to the limit. And he had the very rare and very great attribute of accepting responsibility without underwriting his risks.

That morning he had calmly doubled the stakes. He had left Hazlerigg in no doubt as to the seriousness of the situation. And he had offered him commensurate powers. What he had given him was the nearest thing to a *carte blanche* since the British fifth column had been liquidated in the autumn of 1938. Which made it all very nice for Hazlerigg—if he succeeded. He turned again to the paper in front of him. It was a typed transcript of Major McCann's interview with Gunner Andrews, duly taken down in the next room as it came over the Tannoy speaker connected to the microphones under the wainscoting of that functional apartment.

He was puzzled about Curly. It was possible, of course, that McCann had not noticed the slip, and in that case his failure to mention it was venial. It was equally possible that McCann *had* noticed it, and deliberately kept the information to himself. In order not to incriminate another of his men? Possibly. Or in order to follow the line himself. That was a more likely solution.

The thought made Hazlerigg shudder.

He had taken the precaution of putting a man on to the Major's tail, but this did not really solve the problem. To shadow a suspect successfully twenty-four hours of the day, day after day, needed a minimum of six trained operatives. Even with his new powers he

46

couldn't throw men about on that scale.

It was perfectly possible, for instance, that even if McCann meditated independent action he might not put his plans into operation immediately. He might wait for a week. He might take a month's holiday in the country first. "Take someone to help you," he had said to Crabbe, "and watch him for the rest of the day. If he seems to be doing anything in the least bit odd, phone me straight away, and I'll think about making a permanent job out of it."

• 2 •

McCann had lunch at the Corner House and then walked home across Regents Park. He found that thinking was easier if he kept moving. The first thing, of course, was to get hold of Sergeant Dalgetty. He would write to him. Meanwhile he would formulate a plan of campaign. Several ideas, remarkable equally for their audacity and impracticability, were considered and discarded before the simple solution forced itself on him. He quickened his pace, causing Sergeant Crabbe acute distress, and arrived home with a splendid appetite for tea.

After tea it struck him that Sergeant Dalgetty might have a telephone and he tried out the idea on Directory Inquiries; without any success, however; so he wrote a post card suggesting a rendezvous in Shepherd's Market on the evening of the day after next, borrowed a stamp from his sister, posted the card (as duly observed by Detective Walkinshaw) and went to the local cinema. None of this seemed very suspicious to Sergeant Crabbe and his assistant, nor (when reported by him) to Hazlerigg, who duly called them off, which, of course, was the biggest mistake he had made so far.

Two days later McCann had met Sergeant Dalgetty in the bar of one of the many pleasant Shepherd's Market hostelries. He wished that he could take the Sergeant into his confidence but felt unable to abuse the trust which Inspector Hazlerigg had placed in him.

Clearly no middle course was possible. Either he handed over his information to the police or he acted on it by himself.

Sergeant Dalgetty had been obliging enough to walk part of the way home with him and point out the doorway into which he had seen Curly White disappear. They hadn't lingered to inspect it. It was the north-west corner of the Square, where Flaxman Street ran into it, opposite the triangular corner formed by the 1940 blitz and enlarged by a V2 in the last week of the war.

Next morning McCann walked past the house again, and stopped this time to light his pipe—sheltering in the porch as he did so. It was an Early-Georgian affair. Obviously it had once been a gentleman's residence and it still retained a frontage of some taste and elegance. But equally obviously it had come down in the world, and was now tenanted by no less than five firms who were willing to pay twice the normal rent in order to put Berkeley Square on their note-paper.

The Major scanned the indicator board rapidly. Starting from the third floor he had his choice of Saxifrage Lamps (London Agency); Leopold Goffstein, furrier; The Cherubim Employment and Domestic Agency; and on the ground floor, visible from where he stood, the offices of Messrs. Knacker & Bullem, Solicitors and Commissioners for Oaths. The basement was given over to the Winsome Press ("Books of Curious and Artistic Interest").

It took the Major several minutes to get his pipe going to his satisfaction, and during that time no one came or went in the quiet passage. Messrs. Knacker & Bullem's

Inquiry door remained unopened. No prospective employers plodded up the narrow steps leading to the first floor offices of the Cherubim Employment and Domestic Agency. (They had probably all given up trying long ago.)

McCann rapidly jotted the names down in his notebook, against future reference, and passed on.

He was on his way to visit his old friend Glasgow, at the Leopard, but a thought now occurred to him, and he directed his steps westward, and half an hour later was entering the doors of the Law Society, an august and sociable body which not only possesses one of the finest reference libraries in London, but is not unduly particular as to who makes use of it.

He located Messrs. Knacker & Bullem in the Law List and ascertained, amongst other items of information, that the existing partners were a Mr. Browne, a Mr. Greene and a Mr. White. Leopold Goffstein was featured in the Directory of Directors. He appeared to have controlling interests in several Fur Firms and was on the board of three Turning and Pressing businesses and Megalosaurus Milk Bars Ltd. Saxifrage Lamps were a Birmingham firm and looked solid. The *Authors' and Artists' Year Book* dealt with the Winsome Press, but in a somewhat reserved way. It gave a list of their publications for the year, consisting mainly of translations from the Silvery Latinists and illustrated versions of French writers who, until the directors of the Winsome Press selected them for the English speaking public, had lingered in a well-deserved obscurity. Of the Cherubim Domestic and Employment Agency he could find no written trace.

It is interesting to compare, in the light of after events, the results obtained by systematic police work and the fruits of beginner's luck and to reflect that McCann's notebook contained at that moment more accurate and relevant information on the activities of Folder 26 than all of Inspector Hazlerigg's filing cabinets.

• 3 •

Glasgow breathed affectionately into a glass which had contained a half-and-half of gin and grapefruit essence, and said:

"But why do you want to follow this man, dearie?"

Miss Carter nodded in vigorous agreement. The three were seated in the cheerful chintzy living-room at the Leopard.

"Secret Service," said McCann promptly.

He had made his mind up on this a few minutes before. It was true that his knowledge of secret service men was limited. On one occasion, previous to the Sicily Landing, he and other officers in his Battalion had listened to a security lecture from a stout major from M.I.5. He had been very impressed by the lecturer's manner, and had surmised that his rather stupid façade must conceal a brilliant and ruthless intellect. Later, on the same day, in Mess, he had played poker with the gentleman in question, and doubts had crept in.

However, his present audience were not critical.

"Coo!" said Glasgow. "Secret Service, eh. That's the stuff."

"Show us once again where the house is," said Miss Carter, poring over a street map.

"It's the corner one, in that block, between the square, Flaxman Street, and Flaxman Mews."

"I see—and that block opposite is the one where the V2 landed."

"That's it—now I thought that between you—well —dash it, you know almost everybody round here."

50

The two ladies looked at each other speculatively. What Major McCann was seeking was an observation post. He had argued, and rightly, that loitering in the street was out of the question. And there were no public houses, restaurants, or shops within a hundred yards of the place he wanted to watch.

"Miss Plant," said Miss Carter.

"Lulu, eh? Yes, she might do it."

They again looked thoughtfully at each other and back at the Major.

"What's Lulu got that would interest me?" he asked.

The two ladies appeared to find this remark highly diverting.

"You say," went on the Major, "that she's got a room which overlooks this corner. But do you think she'd fancy the idea of me sitting about her flat all day? It would be embarrassing for both of us."

The ladies regarded him with unconcealed scorn. They considered, their looks said, that he ought to put his duty to his country before his personal feelings in a matter of this sort.

"If Lulu doesn't mind, I can't see what you've got to beef about," said Miss Carter frankly.

"Lulu's a high-class girl," said Glasgow. "Works in a milk bar. Quite the lady too. She always coughs before coming in the door."

"It's not myself I'm thinking about," said the Major weakly. "I'm considering Miss Plant's feelings. She won't want me sitting round in her room all day."

"Lulu's patriotic," said Glasgow. "She'll do her duty."

• 4 •

Actually the transaction caused surprisingly little embarrassment to either party. That evening, by appointment,

McCann went to the Leopard and met Miss Plant, a coruscating brunette of the Bacall school; she shot him the stock look which brunettes usually shoot at prominent members of the British Secret Service, and then became severely practical. She presented him with a key of the front door, of which she appeared to have quite a number—and a key of her room, with careful directions as to how he was to reach it; gave him instructions for dealing with the landlady, should she appear on the scene, and a number of tips concerning the functioning of the electric kettle and the whereabouts of various small stocks of tea and sugar.

Accordingly, ten o'clock the next morning found McCann propped up in an easy chair at a window overlooking the corner of Flaxman Street. The back of his chair tilted conveniently against the wall, a steaming cup of tea on the what-not beside him, his binoculars handy on the window-ledge and a pile of Blackwood's magazines on the floor.

He was wondering where the catch came in. From his knowledge of detective stories and films he had understood that the watching of suspects was habitually done by stern men in trilby hats who stood in doorways in the pouring rain (usually at an interesting camera angle). The great thing, of course, being that they never had to wait more than thirty-five seconds for the object of their attentions to appear.

The Major waited for a week.

Every night at six o'clock, having watched the last of the inhabitants of 63 Flaxman Street depart, he would tilt his chair to the ground, wash out the teacup, pack his few belongings tidily away, and depart to play squash with the professional at the Lansdowne Club over the way.

He was a man who did not mind waiting if there was a prospect of something to wait for, as many of his late opponents in Africa and Northern Europe could have testified.

On the sixth evening, something rather unexpected happened.

It was already quite dark. The reason for the Major's staying so late was an obstinate light in the Cherubim Employment Agency. Being on the first floor their windows were conveniently at eye level and much of his leisure had been beguiled in watching, through his glasses, the remarkably pretty girl who reigned in their outer office. In his mind he had already christened all the inhabitants of the building, and she was Laura. Laura had gone home at six o'clock sharp. Mrs. Mop had come and gone. Maida Grannit, however, executive chief of the Agency, seemed to be making a night of it. She had come out of her sanctum, into the outer office, and had spent almost an hour searching through the drawers and pigeon-holes of Laura's desk. Now she was telephoning.

At that moment a car turned into Flaxman Street from the intersection at the further end. Its headlamps were on, but dimmed.

Quite unexpectedly, and possibly by accident, the driver touched off his off-side spotlight. It went out as swiftly as it had come on. The car gathered speed, turned into Berkeley Square, and disappeared.

The effect had been as if a searchlight had been flicked for a moment into the dark recess of the court opposite No. 63.

In that brief second it had illuminated a man, standing in the recess.

And McCann had recognised him.

His mind flicked back over the months. It was the hot August of 1944, and the German Armies were falling back sullenly from Paris. The pace was still quick, but the first mad rush was over. The——Armoured Division was heading for Belgium, with its Reconnaissance Regiment in the lead. In front of the Reconnaissance Regiment, for reasons quite unconnected with this story, was Major McCann in a Sherman tank. The driver of the tank were both bad types from the—— Commando, and the turret gunner was a Canadian Brigadier. They were approaching the township of Marevilly-sur-Issy. Both on the map and from the lie of the ground it was perfectly evident that German opposition, when it next hardened, must centre round Marevilly. The town dominated the Issy Route (known inevitably to the soldiers as the Easy Route) into Belgium. The only practicable road cut sharply into the embanked hillside, before turning under the lee of the hill shoulder. It was a defensive "natural", probably first used by Cæsar when he troubled the Gauls, and subsequently improved on both by nature and man.

Surprised and relieved to find the redoubt empty and the road unbreached, McCann had driven on into Marevilly. The Canadian Brigadier was speechless with rage and mortification. He had been looking forward all day to firing the turret gun. It was just like the Goddammed —— ——Heinies, he opined, to walk out on them like that.

Marevilly was *en fête*; and one name was on all lips. Ulysse. He was of that select and formidable band of men, the real heads of the Resistance, responsible directly to General Koenig himself. Hector, Achille, Ulysse, Diomede, Nestor.

What Ulysse had done at Marevilly was, of course, part of history. A Panzer Grenadier group, about two hundred strong, as yet almost unused in the fight, had been given the job of holding the Issy Approaches. Their commander was a careful soldier with a penchant for spandaus sited in pairs and firing diagonally. Unfortunately for himself he had been carried away by the

54

great strength and convenience of the redoubt. At intervals round its hundred-yard perimeter he had placed most of his men and all of his automatic and anti-tank weapons.

He had completed his dispositions the night before McCann arrived, and since Marevilly was notoriously a difficult township he had taken the added precaution of rounding up fifty hostages, including the wife and children of the Chef de Commune. He had then taken up his headquarters in the town hall and awaited the coming of the British with some confidence. At first light Ulysse, from his command post in a cellar in the main street, had depressed two electric detonators. These detonators were connected with ten separate charges of cordite, thoughtfully buried by him the month before in the redoubt. The resultant explosion had left very little of the German detachment or its automatic weapons.

Ulysse had then gathered his picked fighters round him and gone down the main street in the growing light of day with a gun in either hand, openly, like the true gangster he was. He had shot the German Commander with his own hand and the nerve of the remaining Germans had broken. There had been no coherent resistance. Individual soldiers went for shelter and were hunted out like rabbits from a threshed field.

McCann had seen him that morning, a tall man, but so thick that he looked almost short, with a remarkable shock of hair and a florid, Gascon face. When the British arrived he was almost the only person respectably dressed and not visibly carrying arms.

A dangerous, passionless, disciplined man.

This was the face which had looked up for a second in the glare of the spot lamp.

Another car, turning the corner from the square, had thrown a more subdued light into the courtyard recess. It was, of course, by this time, empty.

55

Next afternoon, about three o'clock, Curly White appeared. McCann recognised his pin-toed walk before he came near enough for him to verify the unlovely face. Curly, as the Major had once told him in a fit of confidence when they were sharing a slit-trench together, not only acted like a bar-room gangster, he even looked like one. He walked down the pavement with the exaggerated dancing walk of a dog looking for a fight. He even had his right hand traditionally in his coat pocket. He turned into the doorway of No. 63.

McCann moved to the telephone.

• 5 •

An hour later, when Curly White again stepped out into Flaxman Street, he found it empty. A woman was in sight across the far side of the Square, deep in conversation with the postman.

Curly turned westwards. The street remained quiet and empty in the evening sun. At the Park Lane corner he almost bumped into a middle-aged lady.

Park Lane seemed to contain nothing more than its normal evening crowd. After a moment's hesitation Curly crossed the road and boarded a bus which was on the point of moving off.

The Major had guessed that his quarry would be especially alert at the moment of leaving the house, and had waited at the wheel of his car, safely out of sight in Flaxman Mews.

Presently Miss Carter, from across the Square, gave him the signal he was waiting for, which indicated that his quarry was turning west.

He pressed the self-starter. A minute or two later a second signal gave him the all-clear and he was racing up Flaxman Street. Glasgow stopped him short of the corner.

"He's not far ahead of you," she said. "Don't turn the corner yet. He's getting on to a bus. All right now, come on—and good luck."

Actually McCann found that a bus was not a difficult thing to follow from a private car. He kept well behind it as it moved, only drawing near enough to see who got out at the stops.

In this manner they proceeded up Park Lane, half-circled the Marble Arch, and turned left into the Bays-water Road. As they passed the bottle-neck of Notting Hill Gate the traffic got thicker, and from the lee of a brewer's dray the Major was able to watch Curly dismount from the bus and turn left into Holland Park Walk, that long and aristocratic thoroughfare which divides the blue-blooded sheep of Holland Park from the lower income group goats of Kensington Gardens.

Some rapid thought was necessary.

The Major decided to stake high on his knowledge of that quarter of London. He turned his car skilfully in front of a blaspheming bus driver, went back a hundred yards and took the sharp right-hand corner into Camp-den Hill. A minute's run and Kensington Hill Street was ahead. He ran his car into the cul-de-sac behind the Town Hall, stopped, and got out, locking the car door quickly behind him.

A brisk walk of fifty yards brought him to the corner of Phillimore Gardens and he stepped into the door of a conveniently placed tobacconist's shop.

His manœuvre, he reckoned, had put him a minute or two ahead of Curly. Provided, of course, that Curly came straight on.

Minutes passed and his heart sank.

The lady who owned the shop was fortunately engaged in gossip with a regular customer and took absolutely no notice of him. He abandoned any pretence of being interested in her scanty stock of empty sales cartons, and peered through the misted window.

At that moment Curly appeared.

Two things were obvious at a glance. The first was that his man was getting very near his destination, and the second thing, as a corollary to the first, was that he had been absolutely right in not trying to follow him directly down Holland Park Walk.

Curly would have spotted him at once. Indeed, he had stopped now, on the pretence of lighting a cigarette, and was looking sharply back over his shoulder.

He was so near that McCann could see the boot-button eyes and the greasy black hair grown long in the few months' release from the army.

At last Curly seemed satisfied.

He straightened up and crossed the Kensington High Street which lay ahead of him.

McCann gave him the length of a cricket pitch and followed circumspectly.

The lady in the tobacco shop abandoned her conversation to glare after him. By his abrupt exit he had deprived her of the legitimate pleasure of telling him that she was "out" of all known brands of cigarettes.

• 6 •

McCann was looking into a shop window. The contents appeared to interest him intensely, judging from the length of time he had stood there, staring at them. He was waiting for Curly to come out of a newsagent's twenty yards up on the other side.

He was in the middle of the maze of solid middle-class streets which lie in the crook of the Cromwell Road and Earls Court. Behind him the backs of the monster Kensington stores shut off the skyline. To the left showed the bulked mass of the Institutes.

When a full five minutes had run by, McCann began to feel the first faint stirrings of uneasiness. It struck him that some shops had back entrances.

The newsagent's into which Curly had vanished stood at the end of a block of five four-storied buildings. In each case the ground floor was let as a shop; he could see signs of a green-grocer's and a chemist's, and the third looked like some sort of antique shop. The top stories, he fancied, were residential, though one looked as if it might be an office of some sort.

After a moment's reflection McCann entered the chemist's shop. This was the second one along from the newsagent's and therefore the centre of the block.

At first inspection one comforting fact emerged. The shop had no visible back exit, and since all five buildings seemed to be of a standard pattern, there must be strong chance that Curly was still in the newsagent's. Why was he being so long?

"A packet of cough lozenges, please," he said to the man.

Had he gone upstairs? Was his destination, perhaps, the rooms over the shop and not the shop itself?

"Anything else I can get you, sir?"

"Half a dozen razor blades, and a small bottle of aspirin, please."

He wished he knew more about the interior arrangement of such buildings. In this shop, for instance, there was no visible means of access to the upper storey at all. Presumably the stairs ran from the back room behind the counter; or they might connect directly with the private-looking front door on the right of the shop door.

"Anything else, sir?"

"Yes," said McCann, suddenly making up his mind. "I want a bed-sitting-room."

59

"Who doesn't?" said the chemist, unmoved.

"I mean," the Major ploughed on, "do you suppose that any of the upper stories here might be to let? Coming past that newsagent's on the corner of this block I happened to notice that there were no curtains in the top floor windows. Perhaps you might know of something to let there."

The silence that greeted this remark lasted so long that McCann looked up in sudden anticipation. The chemist was smiling at him.

"I fancy, sir," he said, "that we have something upstairs that might interest you. Step this way."

Out of the corner of his eye the Major saw the figures of two men coming through the shop door.

5

An Accomplished Young Man

At about the same time as the events recorded at the close of the last chapter, Inspector Hazlerigg was sitting in his office.

Indeed, he seemed scarcely to have moved, or even changed his position, since his interview with Major McCann.

Standing beside the desk, examining a large-scale map of the West End, was Detective Inspector Pickup, a quiet, sandy-haired, inconspicuous North Countryman. He was, by a head and shoulders, the best detective inspector in the Yard and soon to win recognition and a Chief Inspectorship, when he broke the Harrogate child murder case and apprehended Captain Throat (whose unpleasant habit, as the public will remember, was to strangle girls between the ages of eleven and fourteen).

"Magnus" Marr, the oldest of the Murder Squad, used to say: "When I get Pickup given to me I know it's going to be a difficult job."

"Go over that last bit again," said Hazlerigg.

"It amounts to no more than this, sir," said Pickup. "Out of a dozen lines we've been covering in the last months, five have gone to ground in the Berkeley Square, Shepherd's Market area. More exactly, in an area bounded by Piccadilly on the south, Park Lane on the west, Bond Street on the east, and Bruton Street-Mount Street on the north."

He ran a stubby forefinger round the map.

"It's a big area."

Pickup accepted the implied rebuke calmly.

"We ought to have done better," he agreed. "Even as it is, we've got nothing very definite. There was the pedlar we were following—you remember—who gave us the slip in the Curzon Cinema. The stolen car we found in Charles Street. That business with the drunk Italian girl on Hay Hill—I thought that might be promising at the time, but it came to nothing."

Hazlerigg nodded. Pickup rarely spoke at random; he knew something more was coming.

"That man you saw the other day, sir: Major McCann. Sergeant Crabbe followed him for a bit, but you ordered him off. Crabbe mentioned the 'Dresden Shepherdess' in his report—that's a Shepherd's Market pub. But that's not all——"

"Yes?" said Hazlerigg.

"I didn't feel too happy about him," said Pickup apologetically, "so I followed him myself. The next day. Several days after, in fact. It wasn't difficult. He always went to the same place. It was a flat in a newish block, on the corner of Flaxman Street and Berkeley Square. Nine o'clock sharp he'd arrive, every morning. And left at six o'clock in the evening—or later. Of course, I couldn't watch the house the whole time, but I didn't see anyone go in or out of the block—no one to signify, that is. Monsieur Bren will bear me out——"

Monsieur Le Commissaire Bren (known to the French Resistance and later to the whole of fighting France as "Ulysse") nodded silent agreement from the leather chair by the window.

"Then this afternoon," went on Pickup, "he came out

much earlier than usual. I wasn't there, but Sergeant Crabbe was watching. The Major got into his car—it had evidently been parked handy—and after waiting for about five minutes, he started away. Crabbe says he didn't seem to be following anyone. Flaxman Street and the Square were both empty when he started."

"All right," said Hazlerigg, "I can guess the rest. Sergeant Crabbe lost him."

"I'm afraid he wasn't expecting the car, sir. Major McCann had always arrived and left before on foot."

"I'm not blaming you," said Hazlerigg. "You've done very well. I dropped that trail and you picked it up. We'll just remember to have a car there next time."

"If there *is* a next time," said Pickup. "I've got rather a nasty feeling about this, sir."

"Major McCann I know," said M. Le Commissaire unexpectedly. "He is a man of some resource and valour. Discretion, too. All may yet be well. As your General Wellington said, 'Let us not cross our bridges before we arrive at them.' In truth, a difficult feat to perform, even with the maximum of agility."

• 2 •

About this time McCann recovered consciousness. He came to the surface slowly from under the dark waves of pain and oblivion. The clouds thinned, turning first to grey, and then to milky white, and then shredding away altogether. The sun came out about five feet above his head, swinging in great solemn circles, as at the First Creation; then slowing down, and finally stopping and turning into a dusty yellow electric light bulb. McCann moved his head, and immediately wished he had not.

With infinite care he closed his eyes, laying each lid as gently as a sleeping babe into its downy cot. After a minute he felt better and opened them again. He felt cold, despite the obvious stuffiness of the room, and he was suffering from recurrent attacks of nausea; but his head was clear.

It was not the first time in his life that he had been knocked out, and he recognised from association most of the distressing symptoms of concussion.

In a few minutes he either was going to be sick—or he wasn't.

A few minutes passed.

He wasn't.

McCann shivered, but in a healthy sort of way, and sat up.

The first thing he noticed was that his shoes and his coat and waistcoat had gone. Also his braces. He was lying on a camp bed, in the corner of a bare and rather uninteresting little room. An attic, in fact.

Turning his head to the left he could see the line of the roof and dormer. Turning his head still further he realised, with a certain shock, that he wasn't alone.

A white-faced youth, of about nineteen or twenty, was sitting on a wooden chair, its back tilted against the wall, dividing his attention between McCann, a damp cigarette, and a magazine on physical culture.

McCann had seen the ferret face before, but he was unable for a moment to place it.

Then recollection came back.

He remembered his first night of leave, the drinks he had had with Glasgow and Sergeant Dalgetty, the walk home through the quiet streets and squares of Mayfair. This was the youth who had come running past him (and whom, as he recalled now with considerable pleasure, he had tripped up).

The first step, he felt, towards restoring a moral equality to the situation, was to sit up. He swung his legs cautiously towards the side of the bed.

The youth spoke.

"Stay put," he said.

The tone which he employed was the tone of a parent armed with both the authority to command and the muscular power to enforce his commands.

Having said his say, he continued to thumb the pages of his magazine and to draw the last lungfuls of smoke from his dispirited and expiring cigarette.

For some pregnant seconds silence reigned in the attic. The house below was very quiet too. Then McCann deliberately swung his legs over and sat up on the side of his bed.

The youth moved with a speed which confirmed McCann's first idea that he had seen the inside of the professional ring. At one moment he was sitting tilted back in his chair. The next, almost without visible intermission, he was standing three feet from McCann.

He was smiling.

His right hand slid gently, almost caressingly, to his trouser pocket, and came out again, holding a cosh. It was quite the nastiest and most efficient-looking cosh that McCann had ever seen, at least ten inches long, and made of plaited leather over some harder core. From the manner in which it hung, its head was heavily weighted.

The youth said nothing, but continued to smile.

McCann sat still.

The youth moved over to the table, without taking his eyes off the figure on the bed.

"Watch," he said.

He picked up one of the playing cards and tossed it fluttering in the air.

The movement that followed was so quick that McCann hardly saw it.

The card lay on the floor, torn almost in two.

"Now you lie down," said the youth, "and have a nice rest."

McCann lay down.

He knew enough of violence to know that a man who could use the loaded stick like that was too good for any unarmed man.

If he tried to jump him, his opponent could hit him three times before he could come to grips. And three blows from that sort of weapon would finish any fight. A weighted cosh will break the bones of the forearm like a stick.

Besides, how could a man fight properly with his trousers coming down? He discovered that whoever had removed his braces had also thoughtfully cut off the top three fly-buttons as well.

Thinking of the state of his clothes brought his mind back to the events which had led to his capture. He could plainly recollect the sequence up to the moment of his entry into the chemist's shop. After that things had become a bit hectic.

He remembered the chemist saying, "Possibly we have something upstairs to interest you," and then— had he started to go upstairs, or not? He had seen two men coming into the shop door, and shortly afterwards someone had hit him. It might have been the chemist, but he rather fancied not. He was almost certain that the chemist had been ahead of him, showing him the way up the stairs, or pretending to do so.

Was he in the same house at all? The balance of probabilities favoured the supposition that he was.

The street in which the block of houses had stood had seemed a very quiet one. It was certainly quiet enough in his present prison. Scarcely a sound came up, either of traffic from outside, or of movement from inside the house. About half an hour must have passed when the Problem Child apparently tired of perusing his favourite periodical. He tried a few games of patience, but was probably handicapped by having destroyed the ace of spades during his recent exhibition with the black-jack.

The Major affected to be sleeping, though actually he felt surprisingly wide awake.

Presently the Problem Child got up off his chair and approached the bed. He lit a fresh cigarette and said abruptly:

"What's the name, mister?"

"Heliogabalus," said the Major sleepily. He was calculating that if the Problem Child came one step nearer he could kick him in the stomach with both feet at once. However, the P.C. stayed exactly where he was. Possibly he had worked that one out for himself.

"You're kidding," he said at last. "The name's McCann, en't it?"

"Quite so," said the Major. "Possibly you could indulge in a mutual confidence."

"Come again."

"I said, possibly you could tell me your name.."

"Smith," said the Problem Child, after some thought.

"What, not Albert Smith!"

"That's right."

"Albert Smith of London?"

"How do you guess them?" said the Problem Child wearily. "My father's name was Smith too," he added.

As if overcome by this startling information, the Major closed his eyes and settled down to sleep once more. His gaoler, however, had other ideas. He seemed to be in a talkative mood.

"You was in the Commandos, weren't you?" he said. The first animation he had yet shown flickered up behind his pale eyes. "Some mob, eh? You ought to hear Curly gabbing about them."

This calculated indiscretion set the Major's wits working. Evidently they had already connected him with Curly White—and they knew that he knew that Curly was one of the mob—and they didn't mind him knowing that they knew.

There were two obvious explanations of this. The first was that they hadn't connected him with the police, and thought him a casual and fairly harmless intruder.

The second—but he wouldn't think about that just at the moment.

"I suppose," he said, "that you couldn't tell me why someone had to hit me on the head. I mean—so far as I know the war in Europe ended last May."

"Sure," said the Child obligingly (McCann noticed that he had a good deal of "Film American"—most of it some years out of date). "Curly said you'd bin following him so he sent word ahead, and we had the reception committee waiting. Of course, it was money for old rope when you walked straight into the joint and started asking questions about upstairs."

"I see," said McCann slowly.

"There wasn't much time to count the change—you might have been a slop and you might not—so bonko, out you went."

"Quite so," said the Major. "Bonko."

"Then Curly comes and gets a good look at you and says: 'You haven't half been and gone and done it,' he says. 'That's not a rozzer, that's one of my —— officers.' So we ran the hand over you, just in case you were toting a rod or anything funny, but we didn't find a sausage. Then we carried you up here—see?"

"You'll excuse me seeming inquisitive," said the Major, "but do you—er—'bonko' everyone who comes round asking if you've got an upper floor flat to let?"

"No," said the Child (actually he said something usually represented as "Not —ing likely", but his meaning was clearly negative). "It just looked a bit off, you following Curly, and this being the day of the move and all."

"I see," said the Major. He was, in fact, beginning to

see a good deal. He thought that whilst the Child was in a chatty mood there was no harm in keeping the ball rolling.

"You'll excuse my mentioning it," he said. "It's just that I did a good deal of co-operating with our American Allies in the closing stages of the battle—it's not now correct to refer to a pistol as a 'rod'. That went out altogether at about the time of Al Capone. The more modern expression is 'Luger' or just 'Loogue', or possibly 'Heater'."

"Thanks," said the Child.

He appeared genuinely grateful for the information. He did not, however, come the desired step nearer.

After another little pause he embarked on a fresh line of thought.

"Look," he said. "You're going into a room. You've got a rod—a heater, I should say, in your hand. Inside the room there's three guys sitting at a table, and you're gonner shoot them all—see? Well, when you pokes around the door, these three guys sees you, and they sees you've got a heater, and you looks dirty. One guy, he starts to shout out. The second guy, he starts to get to his feet. The third guy, he says nothing, and doesn't move at all. Now which of them three are you going to shoot first?"

He propounded this little problem in ethics as seriously as any doctor conducting a viva voce of medical students; indeed, there *was* something almost professional about the dispassionate gleam in his pale eyes.

"You shoot the man who's sitting still," said McCann.

"That's the answer," admitted the Demon Child, grudgingly. "That's what Curly always says. I can't see it. Me, I'd shoot the guy who was hollering."

"You'd be wrong," said McCann. "If he was shouting for help, it would be too late to shoot him, probably, and if no one had heard his shout, they'd certainly hear your gun going off. So what's the use of shooting to stop him shouting?"

"What about the guy who's getting up to come at you?"

"Most people do one thing at a time. If he's engaged in getting up the chances are he's not engaged in drawing his own gun. The man who's sitting still is the dangerous character. He's probably reaching for his own gun under the table. And he'll shoot better sitting down.

"It's just a question of intelligent anticipation," went on McCann, "like boxing."

This long shot landed in the gold all right.

His gaoler's face broke into what might have been quite an attractive smile if its owner had ever bothered to clean his teeth.

"Say, mister, what d'you know about boxing?"

He jumped into a quick weaving action, feet and hands right and left—unfortunately bringing himself no closer to the Major's ever-ready foot.

"I've gone a bit," said the Major modestly. "Amateur stuff. But we had some good boys in our crowd. Lefty Cusins—Patsy Williams."

"Patsy——! Oh boy, what a dancer! You oughter watch his footwork. I heard he was finished with fighting, now."

This was an understatement, seeing Patsy had left his right foot behind in Sicily. However, the Major merely nodded. He was watching the boy's face.

"Lefty—I never knew him. I knew his big brother—I was glove boy to him once——"

He broke off.

The Major prodded the conversation into life again.

"Where did you learn to box?" he asked. "At school —or picking fights in the street?"

The Demon Child seemed to take more offence at the first suggestion than at the second. "School," he said in tones of the deepest disgust. "I never went to no—— school."

70

The Major was not a very imaginative man. But he had a curious little gift of seeing things objectively rather than logically, which was probably why he was a good soldier and only a very second-class business man.

Looking at the creature standing beside him he saw suddenly, quite clearly, what he was up against. He, and a great many other law-abiding citizens. He saw the qualities and the defects, set opposite to each other in the plainest black and white. He saw the guts and the courage and the quite considerable perseverance—he saw the shallowness of purpose, the streak of natural cruelty, and the dreadful sterilising selfishness. He saw, though yet in embryo, the perfectly natural criminal. After his men had come to know McCann, and on occasions when their mouths had been unbuttoned by drink or the imminence of danger, they had talked quite freely to him about their homes and background.

So he knew things which he might not otherwise have known. He knew that it was still possible, in London or Liverpool, or Glasgow, for a boy to live the seventeenth-century life. If he once *did* go to school the school system probably kept him there—but if he never went at all, particularly if his parents had thoughtfully refrained from registering his birth into this world—well, School Inspectors were hard-worked men, and no system is infallible. He himself personally knew of one man who was still "off the record" since the day when he had deserted from the army in the 1914–18 war.

The unconscious object of these thoughts was now standing quietly, with his head bent forward. He seemed to be listening.

Downstairs a door shut.

Then came the sound of footsteps climbing the stairs.

McCann waited with the greatest interest to see who would come through the door. So far he had observed no one but his present gaoler with any clearness, and it

71

occurred to him that it might be useful, if dangerous, to be in a position to identify a few more faces. The steps were outside the door now.

In his excitement he half sat up on his bed and quite forgot to watch the Child Menace. All that he heard was the faint swish of the leather-covered cosh, and then he seemed to be standing on his head in a pit of the inkiest darkness.

Doctors, when asked about double concussion, usually take refuge in saying that we know nothing about the brain anyway. The first blow shakes up the whole cerebral unit. A second blow within a short space of time may have a variety of effects. It may double the effect of the first, and drive a man near to insanity—or the two blows may neutralise each other, in some curious way making the effect of the second much less than it should have been.

The fact remains that though McCann was "out" in every technical sense of the word, without movement or hearing or feeling, he was still able, in a dim and rapidly decreasing degree, to use his eyes.

Through the mists he saw the door open, and a man come in.

He recognised that he was in the presence of a very powerful and mature sort of evil. A face swam across the narrowing surface of his vision. It was elongated and extraverted as if seen in a distorting mirror. And the curious conviction seized McCann that he had seen the face before.

Then blackness came down like a blind.

• 3 •

At an unknown time later—which was actually not more than an hour—McCann recovered consciousness.

This time he came cleanly back to the world of light, with none of the obvious ill-effects which he had felt on the previous occasion.

It was only when he got to his feet that he discovered how weak he was, and he collapsed incontinently on to his knees and remained for a few grotesque moments on all fours, for all the world like an indulgent parent playing at bears with his children.

The room was now quite empty, and the house crouching below it was, if anything, even quieter and more still. The sweat was collecting and dripping from his forehead, and falling coldly on the backs of his hands.

His braces and shoes were on the end of the bed, his coat over the chair.

McCann dressed painfully. Unless his watch had stopped the time was eleven o'clock. Carrying his shoes he crept over to the door and listened. After a moment's consideration he grasped one of them firmly in his right hand, and with his left hand turned the handle. The door opened easily.

Complete silence reigned.

Suddenly McCann laughed. It had struck him how ludicrous he must look. The house felt empty—and he had had enough of playing bogey-man for one evening.

He sat down and put his shoes on. Before getting up he forced his head down between his legs and held it there.

Then he got to his feet and walked downstairs. He went down three flights and found himself in a small front hall, remarkable only for the fact that it was entirely devoid of furniture. A minute later he was in the street.

It was the chemist's shop all right, so far as he could see by the dim street lighting.

McCann walked away slowly, in the general direction of Kensington, and as the quiet and the grateful coolness of the night air began to have their effect, so his brain began to work again.

73

Slowly, but effectively.

His paramount, aching desire was to get into bed and sleep for thirty-six hours. But there was work which had to be done. Badly as he had played the hand, he did not intend to throw away the last tricks without a struggle.

Firstly, and vitally, was he being followed?

He found himself unable to say.

His eyes were no help. The night was dark with an overcast moon, and the streets were by no means restored to their pre-war lighting.

He stopped for a moment, but the blood was beating so unpleasantly in his ears that he could hear very little. He jumped as a bicycle swished past him on quiet rubber tyres.

It was essential to think clearly and quickly. It was at moments like the present, as he knew, that bad mistakes were made. Shock and fatigue were apt to make people do stupid things.

But it was really very simple.

He *must* contact Inspector Hazlerigg at once—and he *must not* be observed doing so.

As soon as the problem presented itself in such plain terms the answer became apparent.

McCann took the first turning to the right and started to run.

He was a good runner. Not a sprinter, but an excellent club performer at a mile and over.

Through the maze of genteel Groves and Gardens, secluded Places and desirably residential Terraces he padded, keeping steadily towards the East. Rain had fallen that evening and the streets were black and shining and quiet. He crossed Gloucester Road without seeing a soul, and by the time he was approaching Knightsbridge he was beginning to get his second wind. He dived into the Park, happily railingless at this point, and by-passed the right-hand end of the Serpentine. By the time he reached Park

Lane he was almost happy, though his head was splitting. No pursuit on foot, he reckoned, could have been both quiet enough to escape his attentions yet swift enough to keep up with him. Pursuit on wheels would have been baffled by his detour through the Park.

At the top of Curzon Street he broke into a walk. There was a light still showing at the "Leopard" and his knocking brought Miss Carter to the door. She took one look at him, and then dragged him through the hall into her pleasant little office-cum-sitting-room. Glasgow was finishing her nightly cup of tea on the sofa. Both ladies regarded him in fascinated silence.

"Are they after you?" said Miss Carter, a little breathlessly.

"The devils!" said Glasgow. "Russians, I suppose."

McCann had fortunately a sufficiency of his wits about him to remember the ingenuous explanation he had given to his female aides. It seemed simplest to swim with the tide.

"You mustn't tell a soul," he said earnestly, "but you're right, it was The Ogpu."

He put his hand to his head in a telling gesture.

"My God," said Glasgow. "We've nothing but a poker between us."

"It's all right," said McCann, "I've thrown them off the scent. Now I must use your telephone, and I'm afraid I shall have to be alone whilst I do so."

As the ladies trooped obediently from the room, the Major picked up the telephone, and dialed O.

"Get me Code 060572—it's a private number, I think."

The night operator seemed unsurprised, and in a minute McCann heard Hazlerigg's voice. He poured out his story.

When he had finished, Hazlerigg sounded neither obviously pleased nor angry, but somehow he reminded

75

McCann uncomfortably of certain Colonels and Brigadiers he had had the misfortune to cross in his army career.

"Give me those localities again, please. An office block on the corner of Flaxman Street and Berkeley Square—yes—and a block of five shops, two hundred yards south of the Kensington High Road—wait whilst I fetch a map, please—yes—you turned south, then west. I see—one of them was a tobacconist's or newsagent's, and one a chemist's shop. One looked like a greengrocer's. All four-storey buildings. All right. We'll find them easily enough. Where are you phoning from? —I see. Were you followed?"

McCann told him his reasons for thinking that this was improbable.

"All right," said Hazlerigg. "You're probably quite right. Now listen carefully. To-morrow go to the North Bank Hospital to have your head dressed. Put a bandage round it before you go—spill some red ink or something on it—I'll leave the fancy touches to you. Ask the booker for Doctor Mann—say you have an appointment. That's all. Good night."

Putting back the receiver McCann found himself so tired he could hardly lift himself out of the chair. Gratefully he accepted the offer of a bed and, fortified by a large cup of Ovaltine prepared by Miss Carter, and two out-sized aspirins produced by the experienced Glasgow, he tumbled between the sheets and dived headlong into the depths of sleep.

6
The Pay-Off

Next morning the machinery moved with speed and efficiency.

A hard-boiled young lady in the Out-patients Reception said: "Oh, you're the gentleman to see Dr. Mann, aren't you? Just step in here, please," and whisked him through a door marked "Private". She led the way through two further doors and McCann found himself in an enclosed glass-covered courtyard. One of the small white ambulances belonging to the hospital was standing there. At her invitation he climbed in, and the doors were shut. The most comfortable way to ride in an ambulance is to lie down. McCann lay gratefully on the lower of the two stretcher beds and closed his eyes. In a few minutes he heard the driver jump up, and they were under way.

With its low pressure tires and independent springing, the ambulance moved with a comfortable floating motion, particularly soothing and agreeable to its jaded occupant.

McCann, in fact, was not feeling so hot.

His body was complaining all over in an irritating indefinable sort of way; his head was not actually aching, but something had happened to his vision and he was seeing light and shade with the peculiar super-clarity which belongs to the first day of malaria.

There was also the question of whether the very light breakfast which Miss Carter had insisted upon his eating was going to stay put.

The ambulance was obviously heading for Scotland Yard. It seemed to be going a long way round—presumably from those motives of caution which characterised the whole proceedings. So far as McCann was concerned, the further it went, and the longer it took, the better. In addition to aching limbs and stereoscopic eyesight he was suffering from a pretty acute attack of Scotch conscience.

Nor had Hazlerigg's tone, as heard on the telephone the night before, done anything to comfort him.

Suddenly Big Ben struck out overhead. The ambulance turned right, then right again, manoeuvred slowly into some gateway, and stopped. A police sergeant opened the door, gave him a cheerful grin and said: "Come along, sir, you can die inside."

• 2 •

"Well now," said Hazlerigg. "If you'll just run over what you told me last night, we'll get a note made of it:" He indicated a young constable with a shorthand notebook. "You can go as fast as you like, this boy's good." The constable blushed, thus contriving to look even younger. "Don't leave out anything this time," he added blandly.

"The truth, the whole truth, and nothing but the truth," thought McCann. He'd made his mind up on that as he came along.

He talked for almost an hour. The constable covered the pages with a nice easy unfatigued motion. Hazlerigg did nothing in particular; at very long intervals he jotted a note on the pad in front of him.

At the end of it all he said to the constable: "Do you want any of that over again? All right. Thank you very much. Let me have it typed as soon as you can. Oh— and you might ask Monsieur Bren if he'd mind stepping along here. He should be in his room by now."

The constable departed and a short but uncomfortable silence ensued.

Then Hazlerigg said:

"Did you ever have officers in your mob who were so brave or so stupid that they couldn't recognise *real* danger when it came along?"

"A few," said the Major.

"The sort who would bivouac for the night in the middle of an unmarked minefield, and get away with it, or stand about lighting a pipe when shells were bracketing the position just to show how little *they* cared?"

"I've met them."

"And did you," asked Hazlerigg, "ever have the job of telling them what bloody fools you thought they were?"

"Yes," said McCann, "but I doubt whether I did it as nicely as you are."

The Inspector smiled and the atmosphere grew a few degrees less frigid.

"All right. So long as you realise you ought to be under arrest for constructive obstruction of the police."

"I realise that I should have told you about Curly, Inspector. It was very wrong of me, and I'm prepared to be very penitent. But don't you think it would increase my punishment," the Major added cunningly, "if you were to tell me exactly *what* I have to be penitent about —the full strength of it, I mean."

Hazlerigg's light grey eyes viewed the speaker dispassionately.

"I'll bring you up to date," he said at last, "on one condition."

"I can guess the condition, and I agree to it."

"All right—if I have your promise that you won't move in this matter *in any way* without my permission, I'll—well, I'll endeavour to bring home to you the enormity of your offence. As you've probably guessed, Curly wasn't the worst of your suppressions. It was that house in Flaxman Street that made us sit up all last night. Ever since you telephoned I've had a dozen men working on the records of those firms. It hasn't been easy, because we've had to work solely by the book, but I think the results are beginning to add up to something now. By eight o'clock this morning the pointer was hovering between Saxifrage Lamps and Mr. Leopold Goffstein, the fur expert. The lines have been buzzing to Birmingham this morning, and I must confess we were beginning to get ideas about Saxifrage. There *are* several odd points about them and I still think that there's some dirty linen in their cupboard. Only it's not our sort of dirty linen, if you see what I mean. I fancy they're rigging a price-control ramp. However, ten minutes before you arrived, we clicked."

He paused, and turned over some papers on his desk. "This report came in. One of our City men has unearthed the fact that Leopold Goffstein controls, amongst other things, a number of all-night restaurants. One in particular, behind Leicester Square, called 'The Bandbox'. He does it by a complicated system of proxy share holding, working through his Milk Bar outfit. Well—the Bandbox is hot. That was where we caught your chap Andrews with the stuff on him——"

"Do you think Goffstein could be the Big Boy himself?" said the Major. "If so, I might be able to recognise him."

"It's possible, of course. But not very likely. I rather

80

think that Leopold is their Post Office—a crowd that's run on the sort of system that these boys use has got to have a safe and easy set of contacts. And Leopold's well placed to do it. His business interests are so wide that he could put a finger on almost anyone from the Archbishop of Canterbury to Goering's niece, without moving outside his own manor. I've got great hopes of Leopold—if we can manage to watch without shaking the web. I'm taking a leaf out of the book of our friends across the Atlantic and we're rigging a tele-camera in a window across the way from his office. From now on we'll have a film record of every man and woman who goes into those buildings."

The slight implied rebuke in this did not escape McCann, and he wondered ruefully what secrets a film of the previous week might not have shown.

"So much for that end," went on the Inspector. "The Kensington show is not so promising. We found the building all right, and the set-up is a rather curious one. About two years ago, when the blitz was starting up again and London house property wasn't exactly booming, a certain Mr. Robinson—a close friend, no doubt, of your young Mr. Smith—bought the expiring lease of the entire block. At that time four of the five shops were let, and Mr. Robinson accepted the shopkeepers as his sub-tenants—but he put his own man into the fifth one, the Chemist's shop. The upper stories were mostly empty and he pretty soon got rid of the remaining tenants. He then had communicating doors cut, at the second floor level, and the doors between the four genuine shops and their own second and third stories were screwed up. What the shopkeepers thought of all this, I don't know. They probably concluded that it was 'something' to do with the Government'. And anyway, he was their landlord."

"I see," said McCann, "a nice set-up. The chemist's

shop acted as a front-door to the whole upper block. No wonder there was a certain stir when I walked into it and started talking about taking rooms on the top floor."

"Stir! I should think they almost stood on their heads. You realise that they were actually in the process of moving out. Had, in fact, almost completed the move. According to the neighbours, vans had been coming and going for days; one of them, who caught a glimpse of the load, said it looked like heavy machinery. There are certainly marks on the floor which suggest that machinery had been bolted down. And I think they had a small blacksmith's furnace—there's a mark where the cowl was fixed over one of the fireplaces. There's no doubt in my mind that this was the place the stuff was brought to for melting and resetting. I guess it may have been the instructional wing, too; and quarters for a small permanent staff. I don't suppose that the Big Boy's actually lived in."

"Why were they moving?"

"I don't know. Probably they never stayed too long in one place. Anyhow, you can picture their feelings when Curly dashed in by the back way and announced that he was being followed! I don't know when he spotted you. Probably not long before. Really and truthfully, I still don't know why you're alive at this moment."

"Since you put it like that," said McCann, "nor do I. I guess that what saved my life was Curly recognising me. He would know that I wasn't anything to do with the police, and the Problem Child told me that they searched me pretty thoroughly and came to the conclusion that I was genuine—I mean, I hadn't got a warrant card or a set of handcuffs on me, and my papers looked O.K."

"I think that's about the strength of it. They may have said to themselves that Curly was mistaken about being followed—it's easy enough to imagine that sort of thing.

82

Or you *might* just have been house-hunting after all. People *do* go round looking for houses. So they decided to keep you on ice till the move was complete and then turn you loose. They were careful not to let you see any faces that mattered. I'm pretty certain we haven't had that boy through our hands. I'll take you down to Records before you go."

"It's a hopeless sort of face to remember," said McCann. "Just a normal, whitish, cockney youngster. The sort that changes every year. If he dyed his hair or grew a moustache or put on a pair of horn-rimmed glasses, I couldn't swear that I'd recognise him even now. The other chap—the one who came through the door just after I'd been coshed—he's different. I told you I thought I'd met him before——"

"Yes—that was very interesting. No—I mean that. I'm not being sarcastic. It's possible that you had met him before. But after all, Major, living in London, and having just come out of the army—well; you must have met and talked to hundreds and thousands of men recently—army types, men in other services, club friends, business friends—even more casual acquaintances—bus conductors, shop assistants——" He broke off as McCann didn't seem to be listening.

Abruptly the Major came back to earth. "I'm sorry," he said, "but as you were talking it came quite tantalisingly into my mind where I *had* seen that chap before. But it's no good. It's gone. Look here, I mustn't take up any more of your time, but there is one last question I'd like to put."

"Fire ahead."

"Well, it seems a silly thing to say, but in view of all this secrecy this morning, and in view of one or two things you've said—and still more, one or two things you've rather carefully refrained from saying; do you think that I'm still in any danger?"

When Hazlerigg didn't answer at once McCann flushed slightly and went on hurriedly:

"Don't get me wrong. I'm not complaining. After all, I asked for it. What I want to know really is this. Do I have to go about with my head on my shoulder and always take the third cab that offers (though God knows it's difficult enough to get even one) and never answer telephone calls after dark, and that sort of thing—or don't I?"

Hazlerigg elected to take these last suggestions at their face value. "I don't think you need worry about any of that sort of stuff," he said. "I mean, I don't see why they should take the offensive against you, not as things stand. That's another puzzling angle to the business. We haven't been able to connect them yet with any of the professional strong-arm boys at all. London's got its fair share of 'em, you know, and we like to keep pretty close tabs on them. The dog-race protection crowds, the Camden Town Wheelbarrow mob, and the real big shots, the snow-boys. If a high-class outfit like the one we're up against bought any muscle, it stands to reason they'd buy it at the best shop. And they haven't. They don't want to *make* trouble. Don't misunderstand me. I don't mean they're playing Queensberry Rules. They're just professionals. They like things quiet and easy. We've never found a gun or a knife on any of the boys we have caught. But that's as far as it goes. If you start really treading on the toes of the Big Boys, the inner ring, then you'll see the difference. Don't forget that they've put themselves outside the pale already. They've killed a policeman, and they know what that entails. It doesn't affect the issue, but they happen to know, too, that the man they killed was a close personal friend of mine. They can't be under any illusions as to the lengths I shall go to catch them, or what will happen to them when they are caught."

McCann, looking at the bleak North-Sea grey of Hazlerigg's eyes, felt no illusions on this last subject, either.

"Well—that's all there is to it, really," went on the Chief Inspector. "I can't offer you police protection. I don't think you'd accept it—and I don't honestly think it's necessary. If they suspect that you've been working in with us—that might be different. Then we'll think again. Come in."

The door opened and at the sight of the visitor McCann sprang to his feet.

"I see you know each other," said the Inspector. "Major McCann—Monsieur Bren of the Paris Sûreté, who is assisting us. Monsieur Bren will look after you until it's time for you to leave. I thought you'd like to talk to Monsieur Bren, Major. I understand you met in France. When you've finished, Sergeant Crabbe will take you down to Records. I've ordered your ambulance for two o'clock."

After his visitors had gone the Inspector sat thinking for a long time. He seemed rather pleased. As he thought, he scribbled busily. Sergeant Crabbe, whose job it was to clear the Inspector's desk every day at lunch time, observed the results of his superior officer's morning's work. It was a large sheet of white paper, and it contained no less than a hundred and fifty representations of a gallows.

7

Shuffle and Cut

The year ran on, turned the winter's solstice, and climbed slowly into spring.

McCann, like a half million other men, spent his gratuity, wore out his demobilisation suit, and began to get on the nerves of his nearest and dearest. Miss McCann showed no signs of irritation with his growing moodiness. Only once, in fact, during those weeks, did she display any animation at all, and that was when two cast-iron finesses failed and she went three down doubled and vulnerable.

She did, however, at about this time, abandon British Israel (on account of the unwarrantable fuss which the Jews were making over immigration into Palestine), and became instead a keen worker for the Young Conservatives.

Nothing very exciting or unexpected happened—if we except the defeat of Scotland by England at Twickenham—and McCann began to forget the little melodrama in whose opening acts he had been involved. Once, as he passed Scotland Yard in his wanderings, he stopped to wonder how Chief Inspector Hazlerigg and his colleagues were progressing.

He read, and for some time cut out and collected, the numerous accounts of larcenies in shops and burglaries in private houses which were filling the papers, and possibly it was this preoccupation which caused him, one night, to dream rather a disturbing dream. It was one of those curiously realistic dreams in which three-quarters of the sub-conscious does the work while the other quarter remains critical. For instance, he knew perfectly well that he was in his own room, in bed—but at the same time was prepared to accept the fact that a flight of stairs had somehow sprung into existence, ending in a landing outside his window. Footsteps were climbing the stairs, and he realised, with terror, that he would soon be forced to see, through the glass, the face of the man who was climbing up. This, he most definitely did not want to do. "Shut your eyes, then," said the common-sense part of him. Immediately a succession of huge, misty faces began to swim across in front of him. First came his late Regimental Sergeant-Major, followed closely by a boy whom he had once defeated in the finals of the boxing at school—and had not thought about since—and quite suddenly the features dislimned and faded and formed again, becoming the face of a dead German with whom he had shared a slit-trench in Sicily for a memorable forty minutes whilst being shelled by the British Navy.

One of the shells burst very close. McCann heard the crump and actually felt the crash and sat up to find that his reading lamp had fallen on top of him. He cursed, disentangled the flex, and took two aspirins, thereafter sleeping so heavily that his sister had to recook his breakfast.

The manner in which she said nothing about the trouble which this caused her was exemplary.

Rodney Blew lived with his mother, and one elder
brother and three younger ones (and two sisters so
young that they hardly signified) in a small house in the
patchwork of small houses which lies behind the Kensington Oval. The proximity of the famous ground did
not cause Rod's heart to beat any faster. As recorded in
the opening chapter of this history, he was of a phleg-
matic temperament. Nor did he care for cricket. Like
Major McCann, whom he did not otherwise much re-
semble, his favourite sports were running and swimming. He also fought, when necessary. A solemn,
white-faced child, about sixteen years old, he managed
to live his own life on that sound principle exemplified
by the actions of the destroyer in modern naval warfare.
What he couldn't out-fight he could out-run.

The outstanding characteristic of the Blew house-
hold, the dominant factor, as it were, in all its activities,
was lack of money. It wasn't just a question of a shortage
of money so much as total absence of that commodity.
Troop Sergeant-Major Blew, Rod's father, had died in
the service of his country some dozen years before this
story opens. (The two tiny sisters were, as you have surmised, nothing to do with him. They were presented to
Mrs. Blew as a sort of payment on account by one of
her lodgers who had fallen into arrears with his bill).

In those far-off 1930's pensions were not dished out
with quite the same freedom as they are to-day, so Mrs.
Blew had been forced to find some work. This she had
done unwillingly, intermittently, and only as an alternative to actual starvation.

Considering these circumstances, and the fact that
his diet in the home had consisted almost exclusively of

bread and margarine, Rod had not turned out badly. He had inherited his father's tough, well-strung body and not a little of his mother's Borough shrewdness.

Curiously enough his first decisive steps towards crime had been taken for the most respectable reasons. When he left school on his thirteenth birthday (as the result of some shrewd perjury on the part of Mrs. Blew) the headmaster, who had noted his prowess at running, had presented him with a year's subscription to one of London's many excellent South-side Polytechnics. Here, on most weekday evenings, Rod had been absolutely happy for the first time in his life. The fly in the ointment was that everything seemed to cost rather more money than he possessed—the fares to "away" matches, entry fees and subscriptions—even the innumerable cups of coffee in which he and his new friends indulged at the conclusion of a strenuous evening.

Being a direct child Rod had remedied this in a direct way.

His first effort consisted in the removal of the entire slot mechanism from an isolated public lavatory in Battersea Park. This coup had secured him the sum of two shillings and five pence, and from that point he might be said never to have looked back. After serving an apprenticeship on telephone boxes he had just moved up into the more aristocratic shoplifting circles when he came to the notice of "Beany" Cole in the matter of some opportunist "leg-work" in connection with one of Beany's periodic visits to Hatton Garden.

However, all that was old history. Rod was now a big shot. He "went out" about once a month. He differed only from a great many other enterprising juvenile delinquents in that he kept himself to himself and avoided any undue show of wealth. To his family, who could hardly help observing it, he attributed his periods of affluence to luck "on the dogs". A curious boy, older than his years, he neither drank nor smoked. Girls, if he thought about them at all, he considered as talkative, and therefore dangerous creatures, people moreover who for some reason expected you to pay for them when they went with you to the cinema.

He had never been in the hands of the police.

One memorable evening in early February Rod was sharing a table with Curly White in a coffee-stall annexe off the Euston Road. Both were silent and preoccupied. They had been sitting there for more than an hour, when a taxi drew up to the kerb. The ancient driver got out, bought himself a cup of coffee and a wedge of cake, and joined the pair at the table. Curly said: "Hallo, Busty," and Rod nodded quietly and moved along the bench to make room for him. No other conversation passed.

The taxi-driver finished his meal and creaked to his feet, said "Coming my way?" for the benefit of the stall-keeper (who was more than half asleep and totally disinterested) and opened the cab door. Rod and Curly tumbled in, and the taxi jolted eastwards with its engaged flap up.

Half a mile further on it turned south, up the Grays Inn Road.

The time was about a quarter to one in the morning.

· 3 ·

During the intervening weeks Chief Inspector Hazlerigg and his team had been doing a great deal of work without obtaining anything startling in the way of results. Since this state of affairs was not uncommon at Scotland Yard no one had been unduly worried by it.

M. Bren departed to France, and worked his way steadily southwards down the busy demobilisation route;

he had last been heard of at Lausanne. A cable received the week before had announced that he would probably have to extend his journey into Italy. He gave no reasons.

Inspector Pickup had taken charge of "Operation Flaxman" and had haunted the area of Berkeley Square and Curzon Street. Incidentally he and his fellow-workers had secured a great deal of information on the subject of the activities of Saxifrage Lamps, and the London Office of that solid Birmingham firm had received a visit from the Inspectors of the Board of Trade. Hazlerigg had advised this raid, since news of it was sure to come to the long ears of Mr. Leopold Goffstein, and if that astute gentleman had noticed any sign of police activity he might reasonably put it down to the misdeeds of his neighbours rather than himself.

Pickup was not quite sure whether Goffstein knew that he was being watched or not. During the past weeks he had received a steady trickle of visitors. These had been picked up by the all-seeing eye of the quiet tele-camera in the shuttered house opposite. "Stills" were taken from the film and enlargements were passed down to the genius who presided over Records—and all with no result at all.

"You couldn't expect anything else," said Hazlerigg when he was told. "Leopold is Postmaster-General. His office is the clearing house. The people who go there are only messengers. They get letters and are told where to take them. It's too easy. You could watch them all day and they could still pass their letters, right under your nose. You could think of half a dozen fool-proof ways yourself—meeting in the middle of the rush hour at a tube station, sitting next to one another in a cinema, sharing a table in a restaurant."

"I've no doubt you're right, sir," said Pickup, "but I still can't quite see why they should bother."

"It has this big advantage," said Hazlerigg. "It works in both directions. The way that they're managing it, none of the lesser characters needs to know where the Big Boys live. The chaps who actually do the jobs— they are the ones who are liable to get caught, you know—couldn't tell us where headquarters is even if they wanted to. They just *don't know*. If Mr. A. wants to get in touch with young B over a little jewel job in Pimlico he sends a note to Leopold. The messenger who takes it may be quite innocent. Leopold reads the message and gives it to C who knows how to hand it to our young friend B—as I said, he probably meets him in a cinema. And when it comes to the time for B to hand the stuff over—well, vice versa."

Pickup thought this out for some minutes without comment. At last he said: "If it works that way, how do you explain Curly?"

"Yes," said Hazlerigg, "I see what you mean. Curly was an operative—what you might call an outer-fringe man. He did an occasional job, and he was used as a messenger——"

"Exactly," said Pickup. "And yet *he knew* where headquarters was. He went straight there after visiting Leopold."

Hazlerigg looked speculatively at his aide and between them, without speaking, the very first faint glimmer of an idea was born.

"It might be," said Pickup at last, "that Curly was needed to help in the move—to help in some minor way. I mean as a look-out or stooge. They may have thought that as they were clearing out anyway, it wouldn't matter him knowing where the old hideout was."

"All the same, I should think that he'd have pretty strong instructions not to go straight there from Leopold's——"

92

"You remember what the Major said about Curly, sir —lazy and insubordinate."

"That's it. He just took a chance. I don't suppose," went on Hazlerigg, "that the Big Boy would be very pleased if he knew about it. I mean, if he guessed that Curly had allowed himself to be followed all the way from Flaxman Street to Kensington, incidentally giving away Goffstein as well——"

"No, sir," said Pickup with a grin, "I don't suppose he would."

• 4 •

The shop and dwelling house of Mr. McDowall, Licensed Pawnbroker, lies in a quiet street south of the Pentonville Road. When Mr. McDowall had purchased the house in 1937 it had been described as a "desirable semi-detached business and residential premises". As the result of a wild night's work in late 1940 it was now quite definitely "detached", the remaining three out of the block of four houses having been shorn away by a land mind.

This misfortune accounted for some of the structural oddities of the building and had not made the task of rendering it burglar-proof any easier. However, after suffering the amount of pilfering from his practically defenceless premises usual in a district where no very strong distinction is made between meum and tuum, Mr. McDowall had effected sufficient repair to enable him to rest tolerably secure o'nights. His immunity, in fact, had lasted for nearly two years and was therefore inclined to be sceptical when he received as a supplement to the *Pawn Brokers' List* the printed warning which Hazlerigg had been responsible for drafting:

SPECIAL NOTICE TO JEWELLERS
AND PAWNBROKERS

There have occurred lately a growing number of instances of burglaries and housebreaking in the above types of premises. In every case in which the proprietor or his night-watchman have interrupted the criminals at work they have been assaulted and in most cases rendered unconscious. This is obviously part of a pre-conceived policy.

You are therefore most strongly advised to telephone the police *before* investigating any suspected activity.

Mr. McDowall, who was a hefty, if corpulent, Scotsman, had been rather scornful of this well-meant advice when he received it over his solitary breakfast table. Now, however, at two o'clock in the morning, he inclined to give it more consideration. He was a light sleeper, and he was absolutely certain that the noise which had just woken him was not due to any innocent cause. He was alone in the house and the house itself, as explained, was isolated. Slipping quietly from his bed he pulled on the sweater and trousers and plimsolls which old blitz habits had caused him to leave handy by his bed. Then, after a moment's consideration, he pulled the telephone towards him and started to dial.

• 5 •

It was Curly who had made the noise which awakened Mr. McDowall. Careless as ever, he had forgotten to locate the loose furniture in the crowded back room of the pawnbroker's shop, and had kicked over a chair.

Rod cursed silently.

The entry had been easy enough. In fact, it had been effected for them by Busty, who was a kingpin on outside locks. He was one of the curious specialists who flourish on the fringe of the kingdom of crime; he was infinitely patient at "casing" a job and infinitely crafty at finding or making a way in, whether it was an office, a warehouse, or a private dwelling. Yet he never set foot in one of these premises himself. He sold his knowledge and his special skill to the best buyer. Wisely, too, he insisted on cash payment in advance.

Rod and Curly knew from Busty that the only person in the house was "that old —— McDowall"; that he was a crusty customer, but could probably be relied on to sleep soundly if they didn't start throwing furniture about; that he had no dog.

Rod, since his experience in Stumpi's Café, had always felt nervous until he had a line of retreat mapped out. This time it wasn't difficult. The back room in which they were working led into a kitchen. This in turn had two doors. The old one leading out into the court, and a second, a makeshift affair, which the owner had put into the blitzed wall. Rod twisted off the staple of the padlock with the poker and found himself in a sort of no-man's-land of rubble and timber. The low wall, on the far side, looked climbable. He moved up two heavy pieces of masonry to form a step, and pulled off the single strand of barbed wire which adorned the top. Then he made his way back. Curly was working on the lock of the big press, and as he paused to straighten his back Rod told him briefly what he had done.

"Good," said Curly, "and now watch the staircase door. We don't want the old —— creeping down on us." It was whilst he was turning back to get on with the job that he had kicked the chair over.

The noise seemed to hang in the heavy silence.

"Christ," breathed Rod, "that's torn it."

"Torn nothing," said Curly—unnecessarily loud, Rod thought. "It'll take more than that to wake him. And if it does, you know what to do, don't you?"

"O.K.," said Rod. He felt for the handle of his cosh.

• 6 •

The mistake which McDowall made, as he realised afterwards, was in not waiting quite long enough. As soon as he heard the police car turn the corner he started downstairs. In his hand he held a serviceable pick-helve.

Rod heard him coming at exactly the same instant as he heard the police car stop, and without hesitating for an instant he dived towards the door. As his fingers touched the handle he heard the first thunderous tattoo on the shop door and out of the corner of his eye he saw the staircase door open to admit the figure of the outraged householder. At that moment the unspeakable thing happened.

A hand grasped his collar and pulled him backwards, off-balance. As he fell he saw Curly deliberately slam the kitchen door.

He lay where he had fallen, quite still and quiet. Mr. McDowall, standing over him with his pick-helve at the ready, thought from a glimpse at the white face that he had fainted. He was wrong. Rod was motionless and speechless, bereft of power and reason, by cold fury. The whole thing had been deliberate beyond possibility of mistake. Curly—to whom he, Rod, had shown the way of escape—Curly had first pulled him back in a callous effort to get away first, and had then slammed the door in his face—offering Rod as a morsel of sacrifice to delay the pursuit.

He almost blacked-out in sheer, overmastering rage.

Without interest he noticed that there were now three Squad men in the room looking down at him.

"There's one away," said Mr. McDowall—"I heard him go." He pointed to the kitchen door.

Without a word two of the policemen disappeared. The other, an enormous red-haired sergeant, bent down, twisted one hand in Rod's collar and lifted him easily to his feet.

"He's just a bairn," said McDowall, who was a kindly man at heart.

"He's a (shocking) juvenile delinquent," said the sergeant, running an expert hand over Rod's unresisting person. "Brought his toys with him, too," he added, fishing out the leather cosh.

At this juncture the other two members of his party returned to report failure.

"He got straight out at the back, Sergeant," said the spokesman, "must have nipped over the wall. He's well away by now. Left some of his trousies on the wire, though."

"All right," said the Sergeant. "Look after this young desperado." He transferred Rod and strode out. A minute later his voice came faintly. He was apparently speaking on the wireless and exhorting an unknown number of people to "watch out for a man in the neighbourhood of Pentonville Road and Kings Cross, medium height, trousers torn——"

Having passed the buck in this satisfactory way the Sergeant re-entered the shop and accepted a "strong tot" for himself and his assistants. In the general end-of-term atmosphere now prevailing Mr. McDowall even went so far as to offer Rod a quick nip. Rod merely shook his head. He had not uttered a word since his capture— had, indeed, scarcely moved.

He maintained this inflexible, white-faced silence during the drive back to Scotland Yard and the process of his handing over to the Duty Inspector. The Sergeant, who was a man of considerable experience and by no means lacking in intelligence, was puzzled. He had seen plenty of prisoners voluble and not a few prisoners both talkative and unrepentant, he had watched prisoners bluster, and he had heard them swear; he had even seen them cry.

Whilst Rod was being re-searched he watched him thoughtfully; now, as he knew, during the period of re-action was the time when prisoners were apt to open their mouths too wide, the time when they committed howling indiscretions which were so often the cause of so much pain and grief to their friends still at liberty.

Their friends still at liberty!

For the first time that evening the Sergeant *really* started to use his brain. He remembered Rod lying on the floor. He hadn't paid much attention at the time, but it came back to him now that McDowall had denied knocking him down. He said he'd found him like that. And the kitchen door had been shut.

The Sergeant looked again at Rod, out of the corner of his eye, and noted the tell-tale tightness of the skin round the jaw. As he watched he saw him shaken with a convulsive shudder.

The Sergeant got to his feet and went quietly out.

• 7 •

Woken at the uncomfortable hour of four-thirty a.m., Chief Inspector Hazlerigg showed neither discomfort nor displeasure. Sitting on the edge of his camp bed he listened to Sergeant Instone and finally said: "Well done. I think you may have got something there." And he thought for a moment, swinging his legs.

"When the Inspector's finished with him, take him

along to one of the interview rooms. Give him a large, strong cup of tea—station brew—and it wouldn't do any harm to put a drop of something in it."

"I think I can get some nice S.R.D. (N), sir."[1]

"Just the thing," said Hazlerigg. "Treat him kindly— lush him up a bit—but he's got to drink it. Two cups of it, if he'll take it. Drink some yourself, too."

The Sergeant grinned and departed. Hazlerigg started to dress.

Ten minutes later he was sitting opposite Rod in the room once occupied by Major McCann and Gunner Andrews. Both of them were drinking large mugs of tea in a fairly companionable sort of way. There was no one else (visibly) present. Hazlerigg said: "I'm not going to ask you for any breaches of confidence, son, about the crowd you work for, I mean; for one thing we know a good deal about them already and I don't suppose there's much you could add, from your own knowledge, and even if you could, you wouldn't—and I'd go so far as to say that we'd respect you less if you did."

Hazlerigg took another sip of tea and swivelled round in his chair so that he was not looking directly at the boy at all.

"There's one thing, though," he went on. "That chap who was with you——" In the mirror he saw Rod jerk. "So far as I can gather from what the Sergeant told me about to-night's doings, that bloke served you rather a bad turn. In fact, not to put too strong a point on it, he landed you up the creek, so that he could get clear himself. And," said Hazlerigg ruefully, "he *has* got clear. We haven't even a description of him and, between you and me, I don't see much chance of catching him. In fact, he's probably having a good laugh at us right now."

[1] N.B.—This is not, as the reader might suppose, some diabolical police 'truth' drug; it stands for Rum (of naval strength).

Rod half opened his mouth, but Hazlerigg was still talking in the same easy way.

"Now we thought, son, that if you're not much stuck on this chap—and we can't honestly see any reason why you should be—I mean, he's forfeited any claim he may have had to your protection—we thought that if you'd like to give us some information, just about this chap—nothing else, you understand, but just enough for us to put this lad where he belongs."

"I'll tell you anything you want to know about him—anything," said Rod with a savagery which surprised even the Inspector.

"That's the boy," said Hazlerigg. "Supposing we start with his present address."

• 8 •

The time was now nine o'clock. Hazlerigg, having shaved and breakfasted, was in conference with the Assistant Commissioner, Inspector Pickup making a third.

"So that's that," said Hazlerigg. "We know enough about Curly to pick him up for five jobs. We know where he lives, and we know his two latest hideouts. We can pull him in when we want to. The point is, sir, do we want to?"

The Assistant Commissioner, who knew Hazlerigg, smiled. "No, no," he said. "I'm not buying that one. You've got a plan in that tortuous head of yours; let's have it."

"All right, sir. Well, this is how I see it. Curly's place in this mob is a peculiar one. He's an operative, of course; one of their ex-army boys, like Andrews—incidentally, as I think I mentioned, sir, he was a very close friend of Andrews, in the same regiment, and so on. But the two men are really poles apart. To start with,

Curly's got a pre-war record. Blew identified him easily in our Art Gallery. We had him in twice for petty larceny in 1937 and 1938. Called himself Anderson then. Now I suggest that Curly wasn't *only* an operative. I think he was trusted a little higher up. This is only guess-work, but I think he was one of the few people who knew something about the central control. We know that he was at headquarters once, and we know that he carried messages to headquarters."

"You mean," said the Assistant Commissioner, "that our best plan would be to locate him and have him followed."

"No, sir, I don't. For three reasons. First, it's been tried before—you remember Major McCann's effort? Second, he'll be as nervous as a scalded kitten after what happened last night. Third, I don't suppose the Big Boys will let him go near them again. I shouldn't if I were in their shoes."

"All right," said the Assistant Commissioner good-humouredly. "You tell me."

"I shall need your support, sir," said Hazlerigg frankly. "Because what I propose to do isn't straightforward police work; not by a long, long chalk. However, the way I see it is this. Some weeks ago Curly blotted his copy-book pretty badly. He went straight from Goffstein's office in Flaxman Street to H.Q. in Kensington. Worse, he allowed himself to be followed. As I suggested to Inspector Pickup at the time, this can't have made him very popular with the bosses. It seems, though, that they must have forgiven him. Anyway, he was given another job. Now young Blew has told us a good deal about his new job. Apparently Curly has to attend on Tuesdays and Fridays at a restaurant-café in Greek Street—a stage-door place—one of Goffstein's subsidiaries. He goes there to get what our young friend described as 'casual goods', odd stones and brooches and necklaces and watches, which have stuck to people's fingers from time to time and which they are scared of peddling through the normal channels. Apparently it's pretty widely known among the boys that you can get 'a fair price for fancy goods' at this café. That's one thing. The other is about Blew himself. He doesn't know it, but we've identified *him*. You may remember, sir, that when Andrews was pulled in after the Oxford Street job we got the tip from one of our informers, 'Stiffy' Hoyle. Well, we had Stiffy up here this morning and he gave us a positive identification. Blew was the young chap concerned with Andrews on that job."

Hazlerigg paused for a moment to allow this miscellaneous item of information to sink in, then he said:

"Suppose we play it like this, sir——"

He talked for half an hour.

8

Curly Is Liquidated

At about tea-time on Monday two large men, wearing dark blue overcoats and bowler hats, visited a house in Camden Town. The car which had brought them was left in the next street, but by inexcusable carelessness it was so parked that its radiator was just visible round the corner. If any of the local inhabitants had any doubts as to the authorship of this visitation, they had only to stroll as far as this corner where they might observe that the driver of the car was an impassive gentleman in the uniform of the Metropolitan Police.

When the door of No. 17 Hatchet Street was at last opened, one of the two men had a short and apparently friendly conversation with the lady of the house, and the two of them disappeared inside.

The local inhabitants waited hopefully. If they had expected anything sensational, they were disappointed. Half an hour later the door again opened, and the men reappeared. They stood for a moment talking over their shoulders to someone who was standing inside the hall. They seemed pleased.

The first-floor front of No. 19 Hatchet Street, who was naturally in a position of advantage, heard one of the men say: "You'll bear that in mind, Wright?"—at

least, he thought it was "Wright"—"White" or "Wright"
—it was difficult to be certain, and "White" or "Wright"
had said "Yessir" quite distinctly.

The first-floor front retailed this information to a select crowd at the "Hengist and Horsa" that evening.
Everyone agreed that it was queer. For one thing, no
one had any idea that there was a man staying at No. 17
at all. Just Mrs. Courtenay and her two girls. The man
must have come in very quietly and lain very low.
Everyone agreed that they were surprised.

They weren't, in fact, a quarter as surprised as Curly
White had been. When he had seen his two visitors
coming up the front steps and had nipped across to the
window at the back and had observed a policeman leaning negligently against the garden fence, Curly had
given himself up for lost.

He had also been considerably disgruntled. "Ma"
Courtenay was reckoned to be a safe lie-up and known
to very few. He had come in with great precaution, well
before daylight, and was certain that he hadn't shown so
much as the tip of his nose at a window.

He was destined shortly to be even more surprised.

Realising that flight was useless he had come down
into the hall more or less prepared to "go quietly"—only
to be met by a staggering degree of affability on the part
of the two large gentlemen, who introduced themselves
as Inspector Berry of N Division and Sergeant Instone of
the Central Force. The Sergeant even went so far as to
hold open the door of the sitting-room for Curly, who
entered in dazed silence.

What had followed had been the nearest thing to a
sermon that Curly could remember in the twenty years
since he had left school. It appeared that Inspector Berry
had been shocked at the company which Curly was
keeping. Sergeant Instone, it appeared, had also been
shocked. However, Scotland Yard, thoughtful as ever of

the well-being of the criminal members of the Metropolis, had dispatched the Inspector and the Sergeant to reason with Curly and show him the error of his ways.

This they proceeded to do.

They dilated on his war record, expounded the advantages of ploughing a straight furrow, and mentioned in passing that honesty always paid.

"Cor sufferin'," thought Curly, "they'll be striking up a perishing hymn next."

Finally they had left.

Curly had been so surprised that he had forgotten to ask them the one thing that was really puzzling him.— How they had known where to find him.

• 2 •

The proprietor of the Entracte Café in Greek Street (Benny to his friends) took a quick look round.

It was Tuesday, it was three o'clock in the afternoon, and Curly was late.

He was not worried about Curly's personal safety or well-being, but business was business, and two promising customers had already been turned away from the empty corner table under the mirror.

The door opened and a man came in. Benny didn't recognise him; there was nothing particularly remarkable about him except that he didn't appear to be able to read, judging from the fact that he walked straight across and sat down at the corner table despite the Reserved card which adorned it prominently.

Benny moved over.

"That's took," he said mildly, "any other table, mister. There's plenty of choice."

Here he stated no more than the truth. The café was empty except for two builders' labourers at the far end, slowly sipping their coffee at a table by the door.

The nondescript man said: "O.K., O.K., I'm from Curly. He can't come down to-day, see. How's trade?"

"Trade's all right," said Benny querulously. "You oughter been here earlier. Had two boys in here after lunch, looking for you."

"All right," said the nondescript man. "All right, that'll do. I couldn't get here earlier, see?" He spoke with some authority and Benny dissolved into a greasy but placatory smile and asked his visitor if he could fancy somethng to eat.

"What have you got that won't poison me?"

Benny performed a small contortion and producing a tattered menu offered it for his visitor's inspection. The latter was on the point of speaking when a wary look came into his eye. "Who's this?"

The shop door had half opened to admit a rat-like youth in a very tight and very shiny blue suit.

"That's one of 'em. One of the ones I was telling you about."

"Him," said the small man, in a voice in which a perfectly genuine surprise and contempt were curiously mixed. "What's he pinched? The kid's money box, or the gold out of his Aunt Fanny's back teeth?"

The youth, who in addition to looking like a rat, moved with a sort of rodent-like stealth, had by now inperceptibly approached the table.

"All right. Sit down, sit down," said the small man. "And you"—he turned to Benny—"you push off and get some coffee for me and my friend—eh?"

Benny disappeared, the youth sat down, and a short silence ensued.

The youth broke it first. He said in a sort of strangled whisper: "I've got some stuff here. I dunno if you're interested. Benny said——"

"Speak up," said the small man severely. "This isn't

the whispering gallery at St. Paul's. And stop looking like a frightened rabbit. Now then, what've you got?"

Thus encouraged, the youth squeezed a hand into the mysterious depths of his skin-tight suit and slid out a very handsome gold ha'f-hunter watch on a heavy gold chain.

"Nice piece of goods," said the small man. He flipped the back open expertly. "Engraving on the half-cover: 'To Alfred Lord Cedarbrook'—well, well. Relative of yours, I expect."

The youth showed his teeth for a moment in an apology for a smile and said " 'Ow much?"

"How much what?"

The youth looked surprised. "I mean," he said, " 'ow much'll it fetch. 'Ow much'll you give me for it?"

"Is it yours to sell?" asked the small man blandly.

"Come orf it, mister. Of course it isn't mine. It belongs to a pal—'e dipped it last Friday."

"Then it must have been Friday the thirteenth," said the small man, and though he had not altered his position by an inch, nor the tone of his voice by a semitone, the youth looked up in sudden alarm.

"I am Inspector Pickup of Scotland Yard," went on the small man conversationally. "I am taking you into custody on a charge of being in possession of recently stolen goods——"

"The youth kicked his flimsy chair backwards on to the floor and initiated a flying dive in the direction of the street.

The two builders' labourers rose wearily from their seats near the door and stretched forth expert hands.

• 3 •

On Wednesday, at lunch-time, Inspector Berry and Sergeant Instone again visited Curly at his lodging in

Hatchet Street. This time they stayed for a quarter of an hour.

The evening papers, in their Late Edition, carried the following paragraph:

YOUNG BUT MUCH WANTED

Rodney Blew of Kennington, aged 16, who is being held by the police in connection with an alleged shop-breaking incident the King's Cross area last Sunday night, is apparently a much wanted gentleman. The police are now in a position to state that information has been received positively identifying Blew as the second participant in a recent burglary in New Oxford Street. Readers will remember that on the latter occasion a small dog belonging to the watchman, etc., etc.

• 4 •

"We can't lay it on much thicker," said Inspector Hazlerigg, "or they'll begin to sniff the Yarmouth bloater."

"I agree," said the Assistant Commissioner. "We aren't dealing with fools. Do you think they were watching the house in Camden Town?"

"I don't know, sir. I think it's probable."

"I suppose you've got White adequately covered?" This was really a rhetorical question. He was asking as much for his own peace of mind as for information.

"The house is permanently covered, and we've got a fifteen-man relay ready if he moves outside. He won't get away, sir. Not unless he goes up in a cloud of smoke, like the boy in the old Indian Rope trick."

It is worth noting by those interested in coincidences, that Inspector Hazlerigg said this on the Friday evening at eleven p.m. precisely.

A little earlier that evening Curly had left the house in Hatchet Street for an evening's entertainment. He took no particular precautions, arguing no doubt that since the police knew perfectly well where he was there was no sense in further concealment.

Nevertheless, he was far from easy.

Chiefly he was wondering why "they" had made no attempt to get in touch with him. "They" were the ruling factors in Curly's little life. Omnipotent, omnipresent, unseen. What "they" said, went.

It was now five days since he had escaped so narrowly from the Kings Cross job; as he had been disturbed before getting hold of any stuff, there had been no sense in going to the agreed rendezvous with "them" on Monday morning.

But surely, by now, "they" should have got some word to him.

Two days ago he had thought that he had caught a glimpse of Joey the Pole in the crowd outside Camden Town Underground Station. Possibly he had been mistaken. Immediately he had moved towards him the crowd had swirled and reintegrated and it had been impossible to get close enough to be sure.

It might not have been Joey at all.

But then there was that odd incident last night. He had been sitting at the window, looking out at the empty street; it must have been well past midnight, actually nearer two o'clock in the morning; he hadn't been sleeping well—probably the result of sitting about all day. The night had been dead quiet and his mind had gone back to patrolling in France and Africa nodding and whispering together in the breeze and the odd shapes which inanimate things took on at night and the sudden disconcerting noises made by the little creatures of the dark. Like that cat, working its way through the garden shrubbery.

Or was it a cat?

There was something smallish and blackish and indistinct. Something or someone. If the moon would only come out for a moment he could be certain. A car had come slowly cruising past, its lights cutting a dazzling swathe on the road but throwing the garden into contrasting blackness. When it had gone, the patch of shadow had gone too.

Curly had sat for more than an hour without seeing anything further.

Well, it was no good sitting at home letting your fancies run away with you. That way you got jumpy and did stupid things. Take a grip of yourself, Curly, and have a nice pint or two of wallop and forget your troubles.

By ten o'clock that evening the beer had performed its kindly office and Curly was feeling something like his old self again. He was in the "Abraham Lincoln", a small quiet public house, north-west from Camden Town, near Haverstock Hill. Full of Poles and Wops and shonks of all sorts. What the hell was England anyway, —— League of Nations? But the beer was good and he'd had some luck on the darts.

"Time, gentlemen, please. Drink up, *if* you please. Come along now, please. It's past time."

Curly turned reluctantly homewards. He still felt the warmth of the beer and the lights and the companionship. But it was slipping away from him. Slipping fast. At the back of his mind a little voice was saying, over and over again: "Come along, now, it's time, past time, past time." It was echoed by his footsteps as he hurried down Haverstock Hill and Chalk Farm Road.

Echoed by other footsteps, too. He seemed to be surrounded by a web of footsteps. Passing him, overtaking him, meeting him.

Come on, Curly, pull yourself together.

He was passing Camden Town Underground Station now; two hundred yards more and he turned left and then right into Hatchet Street. No. 17 was the end house on the north side of the street. It was flanked on its open side by a narrow lane and a square of waste land. As Curly reached the gate there were two other people moving in the street. One of them, bareheaded and wearing an old raincoat, was just turning the corner. Had Curly been inclined to observation at that particular moment, he would have recognised one of his late opponents at darts in the "Lincoln". The other was a uniformed policeman, who seemed to be moving with great deliberation up the other side of the street, shining his torch into the small front gardens.

Curly was half-way up the path when eleven o'clock started to strike out from Camden Church.

And at that exact moment, without any warning, his world disintegrated into a cloud of white, burning smoke and stabbing flames.

• 6 •

In addition to the two men just mentioned (both of whom were detective-constables of the Central Force) the explosion was also witnessed by Sergeant Crabbe, from his vantage point in No. 16, the house opposite. Since the Sergeant had the best view his account was the most valuable.

"White," he said, "was a little more than half-way up the path leading to the front door of No. 17. The path is of flagstones, flanked on either side by a small privet

111

hedge, not more than eighteen-inches high, and a very narrow patch of grass and beaten earth. I am certain that no one can have been concealed in the garden. I had been watching the house myself for about three hours. The eastern side of the garden is open on to a lane and small waste area and it would have been just possible for an assailant to have approached the garden unseen from this direction and have concealed himself in the hedge or shrubbery at this side. I did not observe any object being thrown. The explosion occurred at exactly eleven o'clock. . . ."

"That's how he did it," said Hazlerigg, "blast his infernal ingenuity. It's hard to blame any of our men. . . ."

"It was a phosphorus grenade, wasn't it?" asked the Assistant Commissioner, "with a remote-control detonator. The sort of thing we issued to the French Resistance——"

"That's it," said Hazlerigg. "We've worked it out—we reckon it was placed in position some time previously—may even have been the night before. It had a drag wire round it, as well as the detonator. I imagine that the grenade was buried in the shrubbery on the far side of the path; the drag wire and the detonator line would lie between cracks in the flagstones, and the end would be buried in the laurel hedge. When the operator got there to-night all he had to do was to unearth the wire. As soon as he heard White coming he pulled firmly, and the grenade came out of the earth or leaves or whatever it was that was covering it, and lay in the middle of the path. As soon as White was nicely on top of it—well, he pressed the plunger on the detonator line—and then ran like hell."

"How soon did they get out a general alert?" asked the Commissioner, who was present.

"It took about seven minutes," said the Assistant Commissioner, "we had two men in the street—besides

Sergeant Crabbe in the house—I don't think they wasted much time."

"There's a report here, sir," said Inspector Pickup. "It might be relevant. It's from the man on night duty at the Highgate Village road-junction. Timed just after five past eleven. He says that a youth on a motor bike stopped with engine trouble at the top of Highgate West Hill. It was a choked jet. And the constable helped him clear it—the whole operation didn't take more than a few minutes; but as a matter of routine he noted the number and licence particulars. Well, just as this chap drove away, sir, the patrol car came up with details of the Alert, it occurred to the constable that a fast motor cycle would just about have made the distance from Camden Town to his location in the time available—of course, it was an outside chance——"

"And the number?" said the Commissioner.

"We checked up on the owner, sir, of course. A Mr. Cocks of Somers Town. He says that he left the bike outside a pub in Mornington Crescent at about seven o'clock that evening—it was gone when he came out at ten o'clock and he reported the loss to the nearest police station at once. That bit's true enough."

"Any record?"

"Nothing, sir. I saw the man—I thought he was speaking the truth myself."

"Have you got the constable's description of this youth—the one on the motor bike, I mean?" asked the Assistant Commissioner.

Pickup thumbed the report over, and shook his head. "It's here, sir," he said, "but it's not much use. Medium height—about twenty years old—white face—no distinguishing marks."

"It was smart work all the same," said the Assistant Commissioner. "We can't blame him for not describing the undescribable. Sounds like a typical cockney face."

113

Hazlerigg looked up sharply. As though this expression had rung some bell in his memory. He had been silent for some time.

"Let's have a look at the medical photographs," he said. The police photographer had approached his task with minute and professional zeal. Curly White, in death, had not been a pleasant subject. The face of a man who has been deeply burnt by white phosphorus is, indeed, one of the less photogenic sights. There was one close-up in particular——

"Where is Andrews being held?" asked Hazlerigg.

"At Canon Row, sir."

Hazlerigg turned to the Assistant Commissioner. "I'd like to have him brought here," he said. "He was a close friend of White's, a great friend, I think. I'll show him these photographs——"

9

The Gunner Tells a Story
and Miss McCann Attends
a Bridge Conference

When Gunner Andrews was brought from Canon Row
and escorted into Inspector Hazlerigg's room he had no
idea what was in store for him. So there was nothing to
soften the shock when the Inspector produced the photographs of the mortal remains of Curly White and said:

"See what you think of this, Andrews."

There was a short silence.

When Andrews had got over his first revulsion he
picked the photograph up again and said:

"Is that—is it Curly?"

"It was," said Hazlerigg, with calculated brutality. "A
bit overdone, don't you think? You know, the trouble
with your friends is they're too enthusiastic."

"Why did they do it?" asked Andrews.

"I fancy," said Hazlerigg carefully—he never departed unnecessarily from the truth—"that they got the
impression that White was betraying them to the police.
As a matter of fact they were wrong; he wasn't."

"The filthy torturing bastard," said Andrews in the
same distant voice. He broke off. The beginnings of an
idea registered. "You're not trying to frame me, are you?
This photograph——"

"Perhaps," said Hazlerigg smoothly, "you would like

115

to see the body. We have it downstairs. Parts of it are quite recognisable."

"Gor—no thank you. I suppose it was the old man who did this. It's right up his street."

If Hazlerigg was excited he managed not to show it.

"How well do you know—the old man?" he asked.

"Look here," said Gunner, "I know what you want. You didn't ask me here to talk about sweet Fanny Adams or drink tea! You want me to talk; well, I'm game. I don't know much, but what I do know's yours. But I'm not talking to you. It's not that I don't trust you, but—there it is. I'll talk to the Major, and no one else."

For a moment Hazlerigg's mind was blank—then things made sense.

"I'll have Major McCann down here in half an hour." He picked up the office telephone.

• 2 •

A great deal of trouble would have been saved and almost everything which happened subsequently would have happened differently if Inspector Pickup, when he answered the telephone, had not been busy with a piece of work to do with a greyhound-doping Syndicate (which has no connection at all with the present narrative).

Consequently, he himself got on to the inter-office telephone and spoke to Sergeant Wishart, who happened to be standing in for Sergeant Crabbe, who was at that moment sitting at his wife's bedside and cheering her up with a confident prognostication that this time it must be a boy. On such small matters do great issues depend.

Sergeant Wishart understood from Pickup that Chief Inspector Hazlerigg required Major McCann's presence at the Yard immediately. He had no knowledge of any special procedure or of any special precautions to be taken in dealing with this gentleman. His reactions were accordingly simple. He looked up McCann's telephone number in the Record and put through a call.

McCann, who was in at the time, answered the telephone and said that he would certainly come down into the Yard right away. It struck him as a little odd that Hazlerigg, after his previous insistence on secrecy, should have risked an ordinary telephone conversation, but he assumed that the police knew best.

The call was also received by Patsy Williams, a native of Cardiff, and lately an ornament of the Royal Corps of Signals. Patsy was seated at a table in a small attic apartment, not many hundred yards distant from McCann's flat; there was nothing remarkable about the room except, perhaps, for the extreme austerity of its furnishing. It contained a table, a chair, and a gas fire. On the table was a D.5 telephone, a writing-pad, a box file, and six ash-trays full of cigarette ends. Patsy finished writing down the message he had just intercepted. He then tilted back his chair. From the look of pain on his face it would have been apparent to an observer that he was thinking. His instructions were that routine messages should be taken down and filed, important ones passed on immediately. The filing box in front of him was full of routine messages—chiefly communications from various religious and philanthropic bodies to Miss McCann, but a fair assortment also directed to the Major, looking rather odd as they had been taken down verbatim and mostly started—"Hello, Angus, old cock, nice to hear your voice again . . ." and finished with a suggestion of a meeting in the near future on licensed premises and within permitted hours.

However, this was the first time, in Patsy's experience, that the police had come into the picture.

He got to his feet and made his way down to a telephone kiosk. He dialed a number and said "Patsy speaking."

"One minute—I'll put you through."

There was a click, a short pause, another click, and a very courteous voice said:

"Well?"

"It's me, sir—Williams. I thought you ought to have this message. The Yard have just rung up the Major."

"Yes."

"They wanted him to come down right away, sir."

"I see. Yes. That's quite important. You did quite right to pass it on. How long ago was this?"

"Less than five minutes, sir."

"Yes—good. Now listen carefully, please——" The voice was that of a competent executive, used to making quick decisions and giving out simple, fool-proof directions to subordinates. "I want you to ring Cantropos at his 'safe' number—you know it, don't you?"

"Soapy—Yessir."

"Arrange a rendezvous for about half an hour from now—somewhere near where you are at the moment. I shall want you to show him to McCann's place. He'll get instructions direct from me. He'll need at least an hour to search the place properly. You are to stay outside and watch."

"Right, sir. What about the old battle-axe?"

"Miss McCann," said the voice, "will be out when you call."

• 3 •

At Scotland Yard Gunner Andrews faced Inspector Hazlerigg, Detective Inspector Pickup, and Major

118

McCann. It was to the latter that he addressed most of his remarks.

"When I come out of the army," he said, "in good old class nineteen—that would be last October—I was at a bit of a loose end. As I told you, sir, last time we had a talk together I hadn't got no pre-war job to come back to. I had a bit of money—back pay and gratuity and bits and pieces from one or two shady pulls on the good old Western Front—nothing to write home about—you should have seen what some of the Sergeant-Majors were making——"

"I think," said McCann without a smile, "that the Inspector is only interested in crimes committed on *this* side of the Channel."

"All right, all right, I was just putting you in the picture, see?" Gunner's spirits seemed to have come back to him—"Well, one day I happened to meet my old china, Curly. He came out a group ahead of me. Most of my money was gone by that time, but I couldn't help noticing that Curly seemed pretty flush—each time he paid for a round of drinks he pulled out a roll of notes —blimey, as big as a Brigadier's pay—and of course I asked him where it all came from—not that I was in much doubt about it, because I knew Curly pretty well. Curly didn't tell me much, not then, just enough to make me keen, and a few nights later he introduced me to a man."

His audience stirred in unison. The faintest ripple of movement, instantly suppressed.

"This man was a dago of some sort—a nasty, hefty lump like one-and-tuppence worth of someone's meat ration, with a sump-full of oil on his hair——"

"Just a minute," said Hazlerigg. "When you say dago, do you mean a Spaniard or an Italian?"

"Spanish or Portuguese. Not an Iti, I don't think."

"Thank you, please go on. Where did you meet him?"

"It was a little café—I forget the name now—behind Leicester Square. We had a cup of coffee together, Curly and this Dago and me. And he asked me if I was game for a job. I got to hand it to him—he didn't pull any punches. Housebreaking and shopbreaking, he said. The organisation and staff work to be done by them—the donkey work to be done by us. Just like the army all over again."

"Only better pay," suggested Hazlerigg.

"That's right, sir—thirty to fifty pounds a job, according to the over-all takings, and two hundred to the wife and family if we went down. Well, after that nothing happened at all for about two months. I think Curly did a job or two during that time, anyway he had plenty of cash. Then one evening—at the back end of January, that would be—I got a call on the blower. Oh, I forgot to tell you, everyone who works for this mob has got a 'safe' telephone number—I don't mean the telephone in their own house, in fact, usually not. In my case it was a phone belonging to the bloke who kept a shop two along from where I lived. The mob fixed matters up with him somehow and when they wanted me they used to ring up and he would come across and get hold of me. It was a strictly one-way arrangement. I couldn't call them up—in fact, I didn't know any number to call.

"Anyway—that evening someone calls me up and says: 'Hello, Andrews—are you free to-night?' They didn't give any name, but of course I knew who it was: Why? 'Cos no one else was wise to this phoning arrangement.

" 'O.K.,' I said. 'When and where?'

" 'Now,' they said. 'Right away. Be at Green Park Underground Station in twenty minutes.'

120

" 'Twenty minutes,' I said. 'That's cutting it a bit fine, isn't it? I shan't even have time to get back to my place and pick up a hat and coat, and anyway, it takes more than twenty minutes on the bus at this time in the evening—be reasonable.'

" 'Do what you're told,' said the voice—he sounded a bit narked. 'You won't need a hat or a coat. And take a taxi. You'll pick one up at the end of the road. We'll be expecting you. Good-bye; Clunk!' Just like that. Well, I thought, it's a queer way of doing business, but in for a penny in for a pound. I stepped right out of the shop and there—ten yards up, just turning the corner, was an empty taxi. Here's a bit of luck, I thought, and hopped in—of course it wasn't luck really. I'm just telling you what I thought."

"Quite so," said Hazlerigg patiently. "I suppose the taxi belonged to the crowd you were working for."

"That's right—I got to know the old bird who was driving it later, he was one of their regulars. Well, twenty minutes later to the dot, I turned up at the Underground Station and the taxi driver—that's the first time I tumbled to it he must be in on the game—wouldn't take any fare—he just pointed to a kid who was standing beside the Station entrance and said: 'That's the person who wants you,' and drove away.

"Well, then, this kid——"

"Can you describe him, please?" said Hazlerigg.

Andrews looked a bit blank at this simple request.

"There isn't much to describe," he said at last. "Don't think I'm trying to hold anything up—he had a plain sort of face, young, but tough looking—rather white. I thought he must be about twenty—perhaps a bit less. He certainly talked tough——"

Here McCann interrupted.

"Did he use a lot of American expressions—I don't mean that he was a Yank, but the sort of stuff he might have picked up by going to the films?"

"That's quite right," said Gunner, "he did. That's what I meant when I said he talked tough. Well, to cut a long story short, we did a job together that night—I expect you've got the details here," he added with a grin. "It was a little office near the Angel, we took the safe away on a porter's hand trolley. I never saw what was inside the safe, but judging from the newspapers next morning the old boy must have been in the money-lending line. We just dumped it in the taxi— not the one that took me to Green Park, another one. Softest job I ever had any part of. It didn't take above ten minutes from the time we broke open the passage window at the back to the time we opened the front door from the inside and wheeled the safe out into the street. Ten seconds to hoist it into the taxi, and bob's your uncle! The kid faded out and I walked quietly home to kip. Got fifty pounds for that job; came by post the next morning, in one pound notes. I burnt the envelope as soon as I got the money—according to instructions; and paid half the cash into my Savings account—the one I had opened for my gratuity—and most of the rest I used to pay a few bills; I told people I'd had a bit of luck on the dogs.

"Well, that's how it went every time, smooth as clockwork—barring that last unfortunate bull-up which you gentlemen know of. I did four jobs all told. The second was like the first—an office job. I met the same kid—at Leicester Square Underground on this occasion. The only difference was that I got more warning this time. They were thoughtful enough to ring me up the night previous. Third time it was a jeweller's shop in Kentish Town High Street—and last time—well, you know all about that.

"For the Kentish Town job and the Oxford Street job I worked with another kid—even younger. I called him

Rod—I don't know if that was his real name. I could describe him a bit better——"

"All right," said Hazlerigg. "We've got him."

He ran through his own notes for a second, referred to the cards from the open files beside him and then said:

"The first two times you stole the complete safe and you tell us it was carried away in a taxi so that you don't know what happened to it. The third time—in Kentish Town—you opened a steel show case and carried off a large collection of watches, rings and sovereigns—estimated by the Insurance Company to be worth about £900. That must have been quite a little pile. What did you do with them?"

"We had canvas containers—same as the time you caught me. We carried the stuff in those, half each, under our coats. Next morning about half-past nine we went round to Notting Hill Gate Underground Station and met Curly. We walked out into Kensington Gardens and sat down on the grass—quite safe really; no one in the whole park at that time of the morning barring a nursemaid and a kid or two—and we took the stuff out and Curly put it in a suitcase—where he took it to, I couldn't say."

"The South Kensington Headquarters," suggested McCann. "They were still functioning at that time."

Hazlerigg nodded—he ticked off another question on his list.

"How many people in the organisation did you actually meet, from first to last?"

Andrews considered.

"Apart from Curly," he said, "there was the young chap I worked with the first two times—I never knew his name at all. Then there was Rod, who did the next job with me; and he was the one who was working with me when I was caught. Then there was two taxi drivers

123

—one who picked me up the first time, and another, a funny old stick, who drove me on the two safe jobs. I think I should recognise him all right if I saw him again. No—I didn't get the cab number—why should I? Who ever does take down taxi-cab numbers? And then, of course, there was that dago—I think he was a big-shot."

"One last question," said Hazlerigg. "Apart from the dago—and we'll take you downstairs in a minute to see if you can put a name to him—apart from him did you meet anyone or see or hear of anyone who might have been running the show from the top?"

"We all knew there was someone at the top—some-one running the show. No one put a name to him. He was just the Boss or the Big Boy or the Old Man. Curly talked about him quite a lot but I don't think he'd ever seen him. One thing, he must have been a—what d'you call it—chap who likes hurting——"

"Sadist."

"That's it—that's what Curly said. A sadistic old b——, he called him. He was telling me about a police sergeant they caught and how he'd heard that the old man used his own cigarette lighter——"

"That'll do," said Hazlerigg suddenly and harshly. After a moment he went on: "Anyhow, you're sure you never met him. What about his associates?"

"There was one chap—mind you, I'm only guessing; there was a billiard and snooker room in the City, Curly and I used to go there quite a bit and so did some of the other boys, I think. I don't mean that I knew that they belonged to the mob but Curly was very friendly with a lot of them and it was the sort of place that the boys used to go to—it was in a courtyard off the Friars——"

"Up two flights of stairs and so narrow you wondered how they ever got a full-sized billiard table up there," said Pickup, speaking for the first time.

"That's right."

"It's Ike Shaw's place, sir—the one the Jewish brigade use."

"That's right, too. The place was stiff with shonks. Well, as I'm telling you, I was there one afternoon with a lot of the boys when a big Sheeny came in—and don't ask me to describe him, because I can't. So far as I know there's only two sorts of Jews, oily Jews and tough Jews, and this was a tough one—Benny seemed to be his name. Well, the boys were all round Benny like flies round the dog's dinner—why, Ike himself bought him a drink, and if you knew Ike, you'd know what that meant."

"I see," said Hazlerigg. "And you think that he might have been one of the bosses." He pushed across a photograph of Mr. Goffstein, the fur-expert, taken as that citizen was leaving his office in Flaxman Street. "Does this look anything like him?"

Gunner shook his head. "Never met him."

"All right," said Hazlerigg. "I've nothing more to ask you at present." He paused for a moment in case the other two had some comment, and then went on: "The Inspector here will take you to look at some photographs. Thank you for what you've told us. I'll see you don't lose by it."

When the door had shut behind the Gunner he said:

"What do you make of it—was he telling the truth?"

"Oh, yes—I'd say that was the truth all right," said Major McCann—"as far as he knew it."

"I agree. Anything strike you?"

"Only the simple things which you probably know already."

"Let's have them, anyway."

"There seem to be two, or even three, distinct sort of persons involved. First there's the outsider, like Andrews and young Rod. Only I expect that most of the soldiers

125

were deserters and very few of them went in for it simply for adventure and profit like Gunner."

"Yes; deserters would be easier to discipline—probably they had no identity cards or ration books, and had to live on what the mob gave them."

"And the youngsters would be kept quiet by a suitable mixture of vanity and fear—plenty of ready money and pats on the back and an occasional crack of the whip. Well then; inside them, but not at the centre, are a second group of people, who were trusted further or were in deeper—like Curly and the young terror who looked after me in Kensington. I should doubt if even they knew who the Big Boy was—he seems to have been quite remarkably coy—but they could get to him if necessary through his associates and his contacts."

"Right again," said Hazlerigg. "And I suggest that we know three of this inner ring—Leo Goffstein, who looks after the Information side, and the dago and the big Jew called Benny—it's possible that they do the strong arm stuff. Did it strike you that it may have been those two —or one or other of them—who knocked you out in Kensington?"

McCann considered.

"There wasn't enough time for me to see them clearly, and the shop was pretty dark. All I can say for certain is that they were big men—one of them as big or bigger than me. And one of them, I think, had dark hair—that might fit the dago."

"They're a careful crowd, aren't they? You noticed the precautions they took with Andrews over his first job. They gave him no warning—just a phone message to come straight away. Suppose for a moment that he had been a nark—had wanted to tip us off. It wouldn't have been easy. He wasn't even allowed to go back to his own house—and the cab driver could have seen if he had used a call-box. After the first job I suppose they reckoned that he was well-hooked and relaxed their precautions accordingly."

Inspector Pickup reappeared and said: "I've left him at it—no luck so far."

Hazlerigg went on: "The greatest single safety factor operating in favour of these people is what you might call a certain calculated exclusiveness. Like the British Constitution. Between the executive and the legislature there is a great gulf fixed. We know a good deal now about the execution but precious little about the direction. Some lines are beginning to intersect—that's all."

"And there's always Sergeant Catlin," said Pickup seriously.

"Yes—of course, Sergeant Catlin and a great deal of theory. I believe that what we want now is a little more action——"

With incredible aptness the inter-office telephone on Hazlerigg's desk started to ring.

Hazlerigg picked it up, listened for a moment, and then said, with some surprise: "It's for you, Major—all right—put her through—here you are."

He handed over the telephone and McCann heard a voice so excited that he had difficulty in recognising it for that of his placid sister.

"Angus," the telephone cackled. "It's me—I've been kidnapped. But it's quite all right——"

• 4 •

Miss McCann had been at home when the Yard so incautiously telephoned to her brother and had been much intrigued thereby. However, she belonged to a generation which placed self-control at the pinnacle of the virtues and had therefore refrained from asking questions.

127

Twenty minutes later the phone bell had rung again.

A courteous voice said: "Is that Miss McCann? This is the Secretary of the Ladies' Bridge World speaking."

Miss McCann was flattered but not surprised. During the last few weeks she had been conducting an acrimonious correspondence, by letter card and telephone, with the organisation in question on the subject of the ethics of the Blackwood four-no-trump, five-no-trump convention. The voice, however, was new to her.

"You have shown such an intelligent interest in this matter, Miss McCann, that the Committee has decided to ask if you would care to attend their next meeting——"

Miss McCann certainly would—when was it?

"I'm afraid the notice is very short," went on the voice sympathetically. "The meeting starts in half an hour's time; if you are free this afternoon—possibly you could take a taxi—the Committee would, of course, defray all expenses. We are meeting at the Treasurer's house—14A Royal Albermarle Street in Gospel Oak—it's really no great distance from Hampstead."

Miss McCann would, in fact, have said 'Yes' whatever the distance—she was a born Committee woman. In the cause of contract bridge, she would even have paid her own taxi fare.

In less than five minutes she was on her way. Royal Albermarle Street, despite its name, could never really have been described as a pretentious thoroughfare, and whatever royalty it might have possessed had long since departed. Deeply engaged though she was in formulating her arguments in favour of more ethical bidding at bridge, Miss McCann hesitated for a moment after dismissing her taxi in front of No. 14A. This was a particularly blind and dingy tenement, adorned, moreover, with a notice announcing that it was To Let.

As she stood hesitating, her doubts were set at rest. A

128

well-dressed, Hebraic gentleman walked past her on the pavement and turned into the front path of No. 14A. She hurried after him and caught up with him as he stood on the doorstep.

"Are you a member of the Committee?"

"That's right," said the Jew with a benevolent smile. "Are you Miss McCann?"

"Yes, I am. I was doubtful for a minute whether I'd come to the right place—it seemed such an unexpected sort of house."

"Ah," said the Jew, "but our treasurer is rather an unexpected sort of gentleman." He ushered Miss McCann through the door, which had by this time been quietly opened; following through after her he gave her a most ungentlemanly push in the small of the back which sent her staggering up the hall, and whilst she was striving to recover her balance turned calmly round and bolted the door.

"Take her upstairs, Jock."

Any lingering doubts which Miss McCann may have entertained, faded when she turned and caught sight of Jock. Jock, whatever other parts he may have played on Life's stage, had quite clearly never attended a bridge conference. Born in a Glasgow close and nurtured in a boxing booth, he looked like the War Office ideal of a fighting infantry soldier, gone slightly to seed. He gestured up the stairs with one enormous blackened thumb and obediently Miss McCann followed him. They climbed two flights and then turned into a room with one small window overlooking the street and no furniture at all.

The Jew paused at the doorway.

"I'm sure you will be very sensible, Miss McCann," he said. "Jock here will keep an eye on you."

Jock exposed his remaining teeth in a wintry smile.

"We shan't detain you for longer than we can help—

129

you know what to do, Jock?"

The two men conferred in whispers for a moment, and then the Jew went out. Miss McCann heard his feet going down the stairs and the slam of a door somewhere at the back of the house.

The events of the next five minutes would probably never have taken place at all had not both sides been labouring under a delusion.

Miss McCann, unlike her brother, had no knowledge of violence in its extreme manifestations; any ideas on the subject which she possessed were culled from the politer school of detective fiction in which it was an invariable rule that, happen what might, no real harm ever came to the innocent.

Her gaoler, it was true, was a large and unpleasant-looking man but no larger than various porters who had carried her luggage for her at London railway stations, and less unpleasant looking than a drunken drayman whom she had once put in his place on New Year's Eve in Glasgow.

Jock, on his part, imagined that he was dealing with a frail and spiritless old lady. He little guessed that opposite to him stood a lineal descendant, getting on in years but in full possession of her faculties, of Flora Macdonald, the heroine of Scotland—and a woman in whose veins also ran the blood of a remarkable lady known as "Nut-cracker Janet" who, some eight hundred years before, had disposed of an unwanted husband by melting down a leaden ingot and pouring a spoonful of the mixture piping hot down that gentleman's throat as he lay in bed one night with his mouth open.

As the minutes passed, Miss McCann felt a dangerous contempt for her gaoler arising. That he should *dare* to coerce a member of one of the oldest families in Scotland—he—one of the lower classes (she was old-fashioned enough not to find the term incongruous).

At this point inspiration visited her. Though the room, as has been said, was devoid of furniture, an ancient mirror still hung on the wall. Without moving her position more than a few inches, Miss McCann found that she could see the reflection of the street in front of the house. She noticed also that the front window, though closed, was unlatched.

At that very moment the conjunction of events for which this shrewd old lady was hoping came about. Jock turned for a moment to extract another cigarette from the depths of his coat pocket—and, as she observed in the mirror, two workingmen who had been talking farther up the street, turned and started to approach the house.

She uttered a brief prayer to her illustrious ancestress, and sprang nimbly across to the window.

By the mercy of providence the old sash-cords were still sound.

She flung open the bottom of the window, thrust her head and shoulders out, and started to scream.

She felt two enormous hands round her waist, clung on desperately, gave a wild kick backwards, and redoubled her vocal efforts.

It was a splendid, high-pitched, sustained scream. The two workmen stopped in their tracks. Windows started to open and distant pedestrians turned at the sound.

Miss McCann felt that the pressure behind her was slackening—Jock was clearly losing grip. Having by now secured the attention of a large and growing audience she sealed it by ceasing to scream for a moment and ejaculating the single thrilling word: "Murder."

Even from two stories up she could hear the murmur of satisfaction which arose from her public.

A thud of feet in the room behind her announced

131

that Jock had abandoned the position and was making good his escape.

The arrival of a policeman and the subsequent explanations covered a period of about ten minutes. The policeman, though puzzled, acted with promptitude. A rapid search revealed the fact that 14A was quite empty.

Miss McCann accompanied him back to the police-station, with a section of the crowd still hopefully in pursuit.

From there she rang up her brother—first at the flat, without success, and then, remembering the events of earlier in the afternoon, at Scotland Yard.

10
Rough Stuff

When Miss McCann had concluded her epic account the Major said with unwonted warmth: "Bravo, Polly, old girl—go and get yourself a cup of tea somewhere."

He could sense, even over the telephone, that she was rattled, and it struck him that it would be a good thing if he hurried back and got home ahead of her.

"There's been some attempt to rob my sister," he said to Hazlerigg. "As far as I can make out some blackguard rang up pretending to be a member of a bridge committee and lured Polly out to Gospel Oak. I haven't got the full strength of it yet. You don't think," he added in sudden alarm, "that it was anything to do with this other business?"

"Until we know a little more about the circumstances, it's difficult to say. She was speaking from Highgate Police Station, wasn't she? I'll ask them for a full report. But I don't really see how the two things could be connected—particularly as we've been so very careful so far never to associate you with the police——"

McCann remembered something.

"I *was* surprised," he said, "that you risked a telephone call to me to-day on the public line."

There was a moment of shocked silence, and then Hazlerigg and Inspector Pickup both started to say something at the same time and both thought better of it. Hazlerigg looked more than usually like the Great Protector—in one of his Drogheda and Wexford moods—Pickup was scarlet.

"Oh dear," said McCann to himself. An intimate acquaintance with service life told him exactly what had happened. It was plain that Detective Inspector Pickup was going to be on the receiving end of a thundering departmental rocket, and equally clear (by the rigid etiquette governing these matters) that the rocket could not be delivered in the presence of a third party.

"This puts rather a different complexion on Polly's jaunt this afternoon," he said. "I can't imagine what they wanted of her—anyway, thanks to the power of her lungs, they don't seem to have got very far. I think I'd better hurry home and be there when the old girl gets back."

"I think you're right," said Hazlerigg. "Keep in touch with us. In view of the latest development"—he shot a malevolent glance at Pickup, who seemed to be on the point of apoplexy—"we needn't be so careful of approaching each other. If you want us, ring up my Code number from a public box—or use a friend's phone—your own line's almost certainly tapped. I'll get the post office on to tracing it back right away."

· 2 ·

When McCann reached the street in front of his flat he was still trying to puzzle out the reasons for such an extraordinary attack on his sister. Had They intended—a fantastic thought—to hold her as some sort of hostage? He was so deep in these meditations that he did not notice a shabbily-dressed man busily doing nothing in the hall doorway of the next block to his own; a man who gave him a startled glance as he strode by, and then emitted a piercing and unmelodious whistle of the sort much favoured by errand boys with gaps in their front teeth but rarely employed by grown-up people.

McCann ran on upstairs, seeing and hearing nothing.

Two things jerked him suddenly back to reality. The front door of his flat was open—and beyond it, as he could see, at the end of the short front hall, the living-room door was shut.

Now Miss McCann, as her brother knew, was a careful householder, most unlikely to leave her front door unlocked. Further, out of regard for her sedate Persian cat, she made a practice, when going out, of leaving the living-room door ajar so that the careful beast might have the run of the ash-bucket in the kitchen.

McCann pondered these auguries for a moment and then stepped quietly into the little hall—and shut the front door behind him.

Three or four steps took him to the living-room door; and again he waited.

From inside the room came one of those tiny, indefinable noises which suggest human presence—the creak of shoe leather, the click of an ankle joint, the brush of cloth against a table edge.

McCann turned the handle, kicked the door open, and stepped inside.

At the far end of the room, crouching against the bureau, was one of the nastiest, oiliest, curliest specimens of South European that McCann had ever seen. The opened drawers and spilt contents of the bureau told their own story. A cash box, its lid forced back, stood like a half-submerged rock among a sea of scattered papers.

From outside in the street, three stories below, came another despairing whistle.

"I expect that's your friend whistling to you," said McCann conversationally.

The intruder seemed to make up his mind reluctantly. He straightened up from his crouching position, and it was now apparent that he held a knife in his right hand.

The sight was a tonic to McCann.

If it had been a gun, his tactics would have been subject to drastic revision. As it was, the prospect was simple, enlivening and colourful.

The man was quite obviously armed with a weapon which he had not the faintest idea how to use. It was a Commando knife and he was holding it as a man might hold a date-stamp, with the business end downwards and his fingers curled round the handle.

McCann picked up a solid dining-room chair, canted up the legs, and launched himself enthusiastically forward. He weighed nearly fifteen stone, and, coming the full length of the room, by the time he arrived his momentum was considerable. The chair caught the intruder just off centre—its upper leg paralysing his right arm and one, at least, of its lower legs landing with a satisfactory sound in the more than ample stomach.

For a second the man stood pinned against the desk.

Then his knife wavered ineffectually forward. McCann, still leaning on the chair, kicked hard in an upwards direction. It was not a gentlemanly thing to do; he was not feeling gentlemanly.

His uninvited guest gave a scream like the Flying Scotsman passing through Market Harboro' and the knife dropped to the floor.

Judging the time to be ripe, McCann released his pressure on the chair and his visitor sagged to the ground, where he lay moaning.

Slipping from the room, McCann returned quickly with a leather strap from his valise and a cricket club tie (the colours of which he had never really liked), and in less time than it takes to tell, the stout gentleman— closer inspection suggested that he might be a Greek— was lying on the sofa, his hands and feet tied in a neat bundle behind his back.

He was still bubbling gently.

The Major moved over to the window. The shabbily dressed gentleman had disappeared. All was quiet.

"Here," thought McCann, "is where fact and fiction part company. If I am Bulldog Drummond or the Saint or even one of the Four Just Men, my next step is childishly simple. Here I have one of the other side delivered into my hand. He is clearly a yellow rat. The merest suggestion of the application of a lighted match to the sole of his foot and he will tell me all he knows. He will reveal the name of the Great White Chief and the headquarters of the gang—whereupon I shall proceed to the latter and demolish the former."

Fortunately—or perhaps unfortunately—there are two distinct types of people. Those who can torture a fellow-being and those who can't. The Major belonged, by operation of nature, to the second group, and his convictions on the subject had been fortified by certain glimpses of recently liberated France. He remembered in particular a quiet house in the back streets of Rouen, with its iron rings in the wall and criss-cross channels in the cement floor—a house which no Frenchman would ever inhabit again as long as memory lasted.

He trudged downstairs to the call-box and rang up Scotland Yard.

Inspector Pickup arrived in a Squad car, and his face lighted up when he saw the figure on the sofa. "Why, Soapy," he said cordially, "this is an unexpected pleasure; it really is, now. You're entertaining quite a celebrity, Major. Soapy the Greek. So called from his habit of opening Yale locks with soft soap and paraffin wax."

137

Leaving a sergeant to remove the Major's tie and belt and replace them with a more orthodox pair of handcuffs, Pickup led the way out into the hall.

"That's his trade-mark," he said. Looking closely, McCann could see signs of waxy film across the face of the lock.

"It's really very simple," said Pickup, "like all great inventions. You force-feed the mixture into the front of the lock. Then, next time the door is opened by the householder, all the little spring-loaded tumblers, which normally act as catches, get caught up and stuck in the wax—see? All you need then to open the door is a blank key. They may have done the actual waxing weeks ago— you wouldn't notice it unless you were expecting it."

"They don't tell nobody nothing these days," said McCann. "What does the prudent householder do next?"

"The prudent householder," said Pickup, "fits a mortice lock as well—and uses it. Yes, what is it, Sergeant?"

"I've searched him, sir. Usual private possessions, then there's these three blank Yales on a ring, and I found this knife on the floor."

"Yes," said McCann with a grin, "he dropped it."

"Also this notebook, sir."

The notebook revealed nothing of startling interest except that on the last page there was a memorandum —evidently made in haste, presumably by Soapy himself. It consisted of McCann's name and address—followed by one word—"Urgent". Pickup considered this for a moment solemnly. Then he said: "I suppose that this is what Soapy took down over the telephone—they read out your name and address—and then someone said: 'This is an urgent job, Soapy, a very urgent job . . . !'"

"That's right," said McCann. "What about it?"

"Well——" said Pickup slowly, "if you're urgent to *them*—then you're urgent to *us*. I think you'd better come along down with me to the Yard."

"I've got to leave a message for my sister—she'll be here at any moment."

"Leave it with the constable—he'll be stopping here——"

"All right," said McCann, impressed in spite of himself by this evidence of his own importance, "so long as he doesn't scare the old lady into fits."

Pickup turned to the Sergeant. "Put Soapy in the car—we'll have to drop him at the station and see to charging him. Detail one of your men to stay here. I'll have him relieved by a local as soon as I can. Ready, sir? Come along then."

"So he was Urgent now, was he?" thought McCann, as he finished scribbling out a note for his sister. "Urgent—Handle with Care—Fragile."

• 3 •

Down at the Yard there was a sort of family reunion in progress. Besides Hazlerigg, Monsieur Bren was there. He looked a little tired—as in fact he was, since he had been travelling for the last forty-eight hours, most of the time on his feet. In the visitor's chair there was seated a full colonel of the British Army, wearing staff tabs and the ribbon of the Distinguished Service Order. Hazlerigg effected the introductions.

"Major McCann—this is Colonel Hunt, from the War Office. He's got a job for you."

"Good God," said McCann, "has war broken out again?" The Colonel displayed his white teeth in two inches of regulation military smile and said: "Not quite."

He was, in fact, one of those excellent staff officers

139

produced by this war; brave, capable of working indefinitely for eighteen hours a day, and fortunate in being completely devoid of any sense of humour.

"I have at last been able to regularise your position," said Hazlerigg, and the relief in his voice was apparent. The Colonel looked up and nodded his approval of the sentiment. As an army man he sympathised with Hazlerigg. He himself had spent some of his worst moments of the war trying to regularise the position of numbers of unpredictable territorial officers.

"Monsieur Bren," went on Hazlerigg, "has succeeded in establishing, beyond any reasonable doubt, that the proceeds of these robberies have left England by military routes—unknown of course to the military authorities."

The Colonel nodded again.

"We are not yet quite certain in what form the stuff leaves the country—but it reaches France and Italy in the possession of soldiers returning from leave in this country. Foreign valuables from those two countries are probably coming in on the same route."

"That I have not established," said M. Bren.

"It's a fair presumption," said Hazlerigg, "but we'll let it go for the moment. The point is this. In the near future we shall have to investigate the whole Medloc Leave Line from Milan until it touches England—in particular the Medloc Camps at Dieppe and Ostend. To do this properly we shall need Army Co-operation."

The Colonel nodded once more.

"In short," said Hazlerigg, "we've asked for a liaison officer—and you're it."

"But," said McCann, "I mean—I'd love to do it, but I'm not in the Army any longer—even my demob. leave's over. It ended last month—I'm right out now."

Colonel Hunt smiled the tolerant smile of the expert.

"You're forgetting," he said, "that you hold a Territorial Commission, not an Emergency one."

"Good God," said McCann. "So I do—but I imagined it had ceased to function."

"His Majesty's Commission," said the Colonel, a touch severely, "never ceases to function. You will naturally have to revert to your substantive rank of lieutenant. You will receive pay and allowances directly from us—you have permission to wear civilian clothes—you will act entirely under Chief Inspector Hazlerigg's orders. If any technical questions arise, you can refer them direct to me. I think that's all—good-bye, Inspector. I can find my own way out, thank you. Good-bye, McCann."

"Good-bye," said Lieutenant McCann dazedly.

There was a period of silence whilst the vacuum, caused by the Colonel's departure, filled in slowly.

"Well, Chief," said McCann at last, "what's the next move?"

"My first tentative suggestion is that you find yourself a new lodging. Your present one is a little too popular for our purposes. But, of course, there's your sister to think of. If you go, I suppose she'll hardly like to live in the flat alone. Hasn't she some relations she could stay with?"

"That shows how little you know about my sister," said McCann. "Hitler, Hell and High-water have failed to move her—she won't be likely to shift for a mere gangster. Seriously, though, if I go, I take it there's no reason to suppose that they'll worry her. The point of this afternoon's business is now pretty clear. They just wanted her out of the way whilst they searched the flat."

"All right," said the Inspector. "I expect you're right. Any idea where you are going to stay yourself?"

"Yes," said McCann, "I think I have."

11

Casting Wide

When McCann reported for duty at the Yard the next day, he was experiencing a feeling of well-being and rightness with the world not entirely attributable to the fine spring morning. Possibly it arose from the comforting fact that he was once more on His Majesty's pay-roll.

The evening before he had "fixed" his sister, who, as he had predicted, had entirely refused to budge. "I've got a special job with the police," he explained, "and I'm afraid it will mean moving into lodgings down somewhere nearer to the centre of London."

"You'll be a special constable, then?"

"Something like that," said McCann.

"It's cold weather for walking a beat," said the old lady. The patriotic and romantic impulses of her youngest brother had long since ceased to amaze her. "I expect I'll be hearing from you from time to time. I doubt you'll be lucky to find lodgings, though."

McCann packed a suitcase, selected a handful of his old favourites from the bookcase, and got out his car. After a short drive round the Heath to throw off any possibility of pursuit, he turned his nose towards town. He reached the Leopard at closing time and sought out Miss Carter.

"Why, certainly," she said. "We'd love to have you

here. You can take the back room on the second floor. The gentleman who had it left this morning to get married. One thing, I'm afraid we don't get up very early here. Breakfast's never before nine."

"That's the time I like my breakfast," said the Major. One of the minor irritations of living with his sister had arisen from the fact that she was an eight o'clock breakfaster.

His bed, he discovered, was an involute affair of iron and brass with a basis formed of rigid steel diamonds. It appeared to have been made cast in one piece, at about the time of the Great Exhibition.

He slept dreamlessly.

• 2 •

At ten-thirty the next morning, as we have seen, he was in Hazlerigg's room once again.

He found the Chief Inspector sitting at an otherwise empty desk working on something that looked like an operation order.

"I'm trying," he said, "to figure out the time-table of what happened yesterday. This is the result so far."

McCann read:

(1) 2.10 Scotland Yard telephone Major Mc-
Cann.
The call is intercepted by "A".
(2) ? "A" communicates with his Chief.
(3) ? The Chief communicates with Soapy and
tells him to raid McCann's flat in search
of information.
(4) 2.40 An unknown person telephones Miss
McCann and induces her to leave the
house.

(5) 3.20 Major McCann is telephoned by his sister from Highgate Police Station.
(6) 3.35 (or thereabouts) Major McCann disturbs Soapy at work in his flat. N.B.—Pickup says that judging from the papers on the floor and allowing for a short time taken to open the lock, Soapy must have been there at least half an hour.

"Well," said Hazlerigg, "what do you make of it?"

"Really efficient work, no doubt of it. If Polly hadn't broken away so smartly and phoned me here, I shouldn't have left for another half-hour, and even then I shouldn't have taken a taxi or hurried home. No wonder Soapy was so annoyed when I turned up."

"It was smart work all right," said Hazlerigg, "but that wasn't quite what I meant. Look at the time factor. In particular, what time do you suggest for items (2) and (3) in the schedule?"

"Well, wouldn't that rather depend on whether it was Soapy himself who intercepted the telephone call or a third party?"

"I don't think for a moment that it was Soapy. That Greek was their high-class lock expert. I don't quite see him sitting on a telephone-line all day."

"In that case—well, let's assume that item (2) took place pretty quickly—say two-fifteen."

"Yes."

"Then the Big Boy—though he does seem to be a hustler—would need a little time to think things out and lay on the reception committee for Polly in Gospel Oak. Let's say he got hold of Soapy at two-thirty. Soapy would start out at two-forty-five—and arrive at my flat at about three o'clock. That fits in all right."

"Yes," said Hazlerigg slowly. "It fits in very nicely; but don't you see what it *means*? We know from Andrews that

144

the Chief could telephone to his subordinates, using a prearranged 'safe' telephone number. But this is the first proof we've had *that members of the gang are able to telephone back to him*. Those arrangements *must* have been made by telephone—there was no time for anything else."

"I see." McCann considered the implications. "That rather knocks some of your earlier theories, doesn't it? I mean, if 'A'—who's just a listener-on-other-people's-telephones—can ring up the Big Chief, then 'A' knows where the Big Chief lives, or works, or he could very easily find out—and bang goes the whole idea of safety in anonymity."

"Not necessarily. I think this is where the private post office system comes in."

"You mean——"

"I mean that all calls for the Chief go first to—I think we may say—Leopold Goffstein. Leopold takes the call and either rings up the head man, or else—and this is a more exciting thought still—*he plugs the call straight through to him*."

"But wouldn't that mean a private line from Leopold's office in Flaxman Street to the Chief's house—or office?"

"It would."

"And if there was such a line, couldn't we trace it?"

"That's as far as I'd got," said Hazlerigg, "by nine o'clock this morning, and I immediately rang up the G.P.O. and put the idea to them. I'm afraid they were discouraging."

"They said that such a private line couldn't possibly exist?"

"Far from it. They said it could very easily exist. What they were discouraging about was the possibility of tracing it."

"But, good God," said McCann, "I'd dozens of signallers in my outfit who could trace a telephone line—it's not a very technical operation."

"So you would think—but you've no idea—and nor had I until this morning—what a mess there is under this old City of ours. The London telephone system didn't just happen—it grew; and it's been growing for a very long time. Old lengths of line fall into disuse and new bits are put in, sections are joined up and other sections are short-circuited. Berkeley Square's a particularly unfortunate area, owing to the fact that a Very Important Person, with sufficient pull, used to be able to get a private line laid from his house to his office. And as if matters weren't sufficiently complicated already, we had the Blitz to stir up the mixture a bit further."

"Then you think it's impossible."

"Nothing's impossible," said Hazlerigg gravely. "If the worst comes to the worst we'll try, even if it means digging up half Berkeley Square. The point, at the moment, is this. The G.P.O. say that the idea of a private line is feasible, but it would have to be a short one. A line of any length would not only be very liable to detection but it would be almost impossible to maintain."

"So *if* there is such a private line," said McCann, "and *if* it runs from Goffstein's office, then the other end of the line is somewhere quite close."

"Sounds a bit theoretical, I know. But we've had a lot of pointers to the Mayfair area already—take a look at this folder of reports; you see—Hay Hill, Curzon Street, Berkeley Square, Shepherd's Market."

Again something stirred at the back of McCann's mind.

He knew it was important. A half-formed association of ideas. Hay Hill, Curzon Street, Berkeley Square. If only he could put his finger on it. No use trying to force it. He heard Hazlerigg saying something.

"I beg your pardon——?"

"I asked," said Hazlerigg patiently, "if you'd found good lodgings."

"Yes, very good, thank you. I'm putting up at the Leopard—the one just off Curzon Street."

"Well, that's fine. You'll be excellently placed. I want you to keep under cover and scout round. That's a bit vague, I know. But I've great confidence in your powers of extracting trouble. We may have to send you to France soon. Until then I give you a free hand. Ring me up here at ten o'clock every morning."

• 3 •

That evening McCann took Miss Carter into his confidence. He had considered the pros and cons carefully and decided that the very slight risks would be outweighed by the help she could give.

"I'm looking for a gang of crooks," he said bluntly and without preamble. "I'm helping the police. They think that the gang may have headquarters somewhere in this end of Mayfair."

Miss Carter accepted this change of role from secret service ace to private investigator with so little surprise that McCann was momentarily disquieted, until he reflected that women were mostly the same in this respect. Try to deceive them about the quality of their butter ration or half an ounce of knitting wool and they would be on to you like a knife, but a whopping fundamental lie would almost always go over big.

"What do you want me to do?" said Miss Carter. They were sitting in her private living-eating-office room, and she looked very domestic and practical as she drove her needle through a much patched silk stocking.

The fantasy of the situation struck the Major very forcibly. Here was one of the most efficient police forces

147

in the world, using all its resources, doing a job of work with a picked team directed by one of the most able practical intelligences he had ever met—and there, on the other hand, was a retired army Major (really only a Substantive Lieutenant, he reminded himself) and Miss Carter, a publican and the daughter of a publican.

Talk about the mouse and the lion!

He realised that his hostess's question still wanted answering.

"You and Glasgow," he said, "have lived in this little corner of London for a great number of years and, between you, you must know a great number of people in it. I want to know *anything* about this area which strikes you as mysterious or inexplicable or even novel. *Anybody* who's come here in the last few years who seems to be doing anything they shouldn't. You know how people talk. That Mr. Jones, who has a lovely office but no one knows quite what his business can be. And that Mrs. Robinson who has a flower shop, but sells a great deal more than flowers, dear me, yes."

"I see," said Miss Carter, she traced a complicated demilune with her needle. "It's going to be a big job, isn't it?"

• 4 •

Next morning the Major paid a little call in the Paddington area. He was following out an idea which had been at the back of his mind for some time. The house for which he was making was in no way distinguishable from fifty others in the solidly middle-class street, except that it was a corner house, and therefore slightly bigger than its fellows, and there was a suggestion of an annexe or out-building in the rear. A card in the first-floor window bore a picture of a pink and white youth tenuously dressed in tight black-and-scarlet chequered drawers with the legend

PROFESSOR TRUMAN'S WEST END ACADEMY
BOX AND DANCING

The Major went up the short front path and gave the bellpull a jerk.

A voice from the depths roared: "Come in—and stop ringing the bloody bell."

McCann grinned and obeyed. He seemed to be on familiar ground, for without further ado he mounted the narrow front stairs and, selecting the centre of three doors on the first landing, opened it and went in.

An old man was sitting in a wicker chair, beside a large table which was covered to a depth of about six inches with a miscellaneous jetsam composed of papers, post cards, dumbbells, boxing gloves, press cuttings (in and out of press-cutting albums), signed photographs, bicep-extenders, strips of leather, the bladders of two punch-balls, the portions of several tyre mending outfits, and the remains of that morning's breakfast.

The old man, who was patching a punch-ball cover, looked up sharply. It was the face of a battered, weather-beaten, but still very human gargoyle, crowned with a diadem of closely cropped white hair.

"Good morning, Professor," said McCann, "how are you keeping?"

The old man peered at him and then his face broke into a broad smile, revealing the glory of perfect, gleaming dentures.

"It's Mr. McCann—or will you have got some military handle to your name?"

"Never mind that," said McCann, "and what's wrong with Angus? It used to be 'Keep your left hand up, Angus. Lead with the right, Angus. Hit him, Angus,

149

you clumsy lout, don't tickle him'."

"Ar, you was never a boxer, Angus," said the old man complacently. "Now, I've got some good boys here right now. Would you care to step along and see them? Real good boys——"

Taking his consent for granted, the professor was already leading the way, along a sloping gangway, into the little gym. Two men were skipping with serious intentness, a third was beating the heavy punching sack and sucking. the air noisily between a pair of rubber gum protectors.

McCann watched them, fascinated, drinking in the old familiar smell of leather, resin and sweat.

None of them took the slightest notice of the intruders or deviated for a moment from his solemn ritual.

"Lovely," said McCann at last. "It makes me wish I was ten years younger."

"Ar," said the professor, "you was never a boxer. Just a fighter. Mind that left, Albert. Let the bag rest on it till you feel the weight."

Back in the sanctum McCann broached the object of his visit. He cut out any elaborate explanation—to which, in any case, the professor would not have listened—and said:

"Didn't Franky Cusins do his training here—Lefty's big brother?"

"That's right, he did."

"Well, it's a long shot, I know, but I'm trying to trace a chap. All I know about him is that once upon a time he was glove boy to Franky."

The professor looked thoughtful.

"That's not easy," he said at last. "Franky liked a big crowd round him all the time. Glove boys! He must have had a dozen. You know how it is. Kids of all ages! When a man's winning they cluster round him. It's the glamour that gets 'em."

"I suppose you don't keep a record of sparring partners and that sort of thing," said McCann, looking rather hopelessly at the chaotic mass of paper on the table.

"Records!" The old man chuckled. "Why, I don't even keep a record of the boxers who box here, let alone the fancy boys they bring with 'em. Wait a minute though—I've thought of something."

He opened a corner cupboard and almost disappeared head first, like some aged terrier, as he burrowed into the piled confusion of papers, boxing magazines, fight programmes and news clippings.

After a minute he emerged triumphant and McCann saw that he held an old photograph.

This had clearly been taken to celebrate a victory. Franky Cusins was seated in the middle, his gloved arms round the necks of two bashful seconds. Standing behind were what looked like three sparring partners—one of whom McCann recognised as Lefty Cusins, the boxer's brother and late a member of his own Regiment. Seated on the ground were three youngsters.

"That's my boy standing on the left," said the professor—"seconded him for the title fight—and Lefty in the top row with Spider and Jim Crow."

McCann carried the picture to the light. It wasn't a good photograph and the lighting, such as it was, had naturally been concentrated on the hero in the middle; but the more he looked at it the more he felt certain he had seen that sharp, white tough face of the youngster sitting on the left.

The professor was unhelpful.

"Them kids," he said, "I wouldn't know any of them. Come to think of it, I don't suppose I ever heard 'em given a handle. Just 'Hi, you, fetch them gloves—and look slippy with that sponge, you little basket.' Why don't you ask Franky? He's out of the game now. Manages a pub—wait a minute—he wrote me the other day."

The professor dived once more into his remarkable filing system. "'The Glossop Arms'—it's behind Victoria. Yes—keep the photograph by all means. I'd like it back when you've done with it, though."

<h1 style="text-align:center">• 5 •</h1>

"I think Franky was *trying* to be helpful," said McCann, telling Miss Carter about it the following evening, "but he just didn't know. He remembered the boy in a vague way—it was eight years ago, after all. He said he remembered him because he was so young—he thought he couldn't have been more than eleven or twelve and he wondered how he'd squared his school. So far as he could remember they just called him Nipper. Anyway, I'm sending the photo to the Yard."

"It's a very ordinary face," said Miss Carter.

"That's just it. His face is his fortune. It's so ordinary that it's almost impossible to identify. I'm far from sure that this is him—and I'm one of the few people who've seen him at very close quarters, remember. Tell me what you've been up to——"

Miss Carter considered for a moment, inserted a further stiffener into the heel of her long-suffering stocking, and said: "I suppose that all this is on the level?"

"What do you mean?" asked McCann, considerably startled.

"I mean," said Miss Carter, "I suppose you *are* working for the police. That Secret Service yarn—that was just hokum, wasn't it?"

"Well, as a matter of fact, it was; how did you know?"

"I asked Sergeant Dalgetty last night. He said that if you *were* in the Secret Service you'd been so jolly secret about it that *he* hadn't known of it, and you hadn't hardly been out of each other's sight for the last six years."

"I had to tell you something," said McCann, "and at that time it wasn't my secret. But it's all right now—everything above-board and level."

"Well, it had better be," said Miss Carter ominously, "because I'm warning you. When I start to dig, I start to dig."

The result of her digging was presented to McCann two days later at the session which took place every evening, now, after closing time.

"Here's the list," said Miss Carter. "And there's libel suit in every line."

The Major skimmed through it—it was a most intriguing document and contained six neatly ruled sections:

1. Mrs. Abrahams—Hat Shop, Granville Street —started in 1943—Sells 7 and 8 guinea models for 3 and 4 guineas. Has two maids—both South Americans. The shop has a back entrance in Granville Mews. Neighbours say a black saloon Packard often visits the Mews entrance at night.

2. "Pastasciutta" Restaurant. Italian style dishes and wines. Elaborate Italian "front". Waiters and Proprietor all French. Known in neighbourhood as a "rough" house. There have certainly been several fights in the restaurant—which have all been successfully kept from the police. Meals mostly disguised Army rations.

3. Eustace Orrey—Commission Agent—Office in Smith Street, upper floor front. No one knows what he takes commissions for. G. says certainly not horse-racing. The office was opened in 1940 and neighbours can remember a lot of "electrical gadgets" going up. Works very late at night. No housekeeper. Has a wireless but no wireless licence.

4. A shop and living-rooms in basement of No. 17 Gt. Galley Street. Shop not now used as a shop

and the windows have been boarded up. Used intermittently by "two or three men", all of military
age, but none of them in uniform. (D. was told
that it was a small factory which made aeroplane
parts during the war—now turned over to metal
clips and fasteners. No machinery ever heard by
other users of building—our informant lives on
the floor above—but several times trouble caused
by blowing of all house fuses.)

5. The "If Winter Comes" Public House in Tovey
Street. Proprietor, Albert Smiles. A "Free" house.
Present proprietor purchased last year. D. was told by
the Manager of The Cock (opposite) that Albert
Smiles is a suspicious character, and alleges:

(1) He is an undischarged bankrupt.

(2) Caters for private parties after hours.

(3) Allows prostitutes to solicit in his saloon bar.

6. The Atomic Club. Opened six months ago.
Manageress—Mrs. Purcell. Occupies premises of
the old Pegasus. Nothing much known against it
except that G. says its head waiter is a man called
Samson (known as the Screw) who has had a hand
in almost every shady dive in the West End in the
past twenty-five years.

"I suppose," groaned McCann, "that 'G.' is Glasgow.
Who the hell is 'D.'?"

"Sergeant Dalgetty, of course," said Miss Carter,
composedly. "He's been most useful. Have some sense,
Angus. I couldn't go into some of those places myself.
I'm sure he'll be the soul of discretion."

· 6 ·

When Hazlerigg read this list at the Yard next morning,
he said: "Good God," which was quite a violent expletive

for him, and forwarded a copy to Pickup for his comments. Inspector Pickup read it through and said: "I don't know why we trouble to finance a Criminal Investigation Department," and sat down and wrote an urgent reply.

No. 1. Not known to us—sounds a bit like White Slave Traffic. May be black market in clothing coupons. Will investigate.

No. 2. This is O.K. The restaurant was used throughout the war as H.Q. of F.F.I. Hence Army rations. Will probably be closed shortly.

No. 3. A crank. Invents things which he tries to sell to the War Office. I'll tell the Post Office about his wireless licence.

No. 4. LAY OFF THIS—We know all about them. No connection with present job. Coining and other offences. Will shortly be closed down.

No. 5. I expect this is a plain case of professional jealousy.

No. 6. Not known to us—will investigate.

This reply was read by the committee at the Leopard.

"I think we might have a look at Number One and Number Six for ourselves," said McCann. "Why should they have all the fun."

This suggestion was carried enthusiastically and a number of ideas were produced to carry it into effect, none of them remarkable for their practicability.

The final conclusion was that McCann should visit the hat shop, whilst Sergeant Dalgetty and Glasgow made a preliminary reconnaissance at the Atomic Club.

At this point they were interrupted. One of the barmaids knocked on the sanctum door and thrust in a neatly permed head.

"It's that young man again, Miss Carter, that Ronnie."

"Oh, God, not the tulip!"

"I'm afraid so, Miss Carter. He's upsetting the customers."

Sergeant Dalgetty, who seemed to have taken naturally to the role of "chucker-out", climbed to his feet.

"Leave him to me, mem," he said.

McCann, following from curiosity, had a glimpse through the half-open door behind the bar of a pallid youth with long and rather mouse-eaten blonde hair, dressed in dove grey flannels with a wasp waist and a canary coloured polo-necked sweater. His high and affected voice floated above the babel of the bar. He seemed to be forcing his attention on two men who had just finished playing darts.

"What about a lovely game of Round the Clock?" he fluted.

"Round the mulberry bush," said one of the men. "You push off, Ronnie, and play tiddley-winks with your own pals."

"Really," said the young man petulantly. "How too sordid."

Sergeant Dalgetty was by now approaching and he eyed him hopefully.

"Come on, chum," said the Sergeant, grasping him expertly above the elbow. "I've got a secret to tell you."

"What—not something frightfully filthy?"

"That's right," said Sergeant Dalgetty, "it's so filthy" —he started to move towards the door and the crowd grinned and made way for him—"that there's only one place to hear it"—the young man was driven apparently quite effortlessly in front of him—"and that's the gutter." The door opened and the youth disappeared.

156

12

Fun at the Atomic Club

McCann's interview with Mrs. Abrahams was not a staggering success, though it produced one unexpected result. He wore, for the occasion, the flashiest suit in his not very imaginative wardrobe, a pair of reversed calf shoes, and a frankly horrible tie (green with small yellow fox-terriers) which had not seen the light of day since it first left its Christmas wrappings.

Mrs. Abrahams, a compact Jewess, dominated the conversation from the start.

"A hat—but certainly—had the gentleman any particular model in mind? Or perhaps he could describe the lady for whom he was purchasing. His wife? Ah, he was not yet married. He must hurry up, mustn't he, before all the nice girls were taken. His fiancée, then?"

"Yes, yes," said McCann desperately, "my fiancée. Such a dear girl—quite *petite*, though."

"And what was her favourite colour?"

"Apple-green," said McCann.

"Ah, she is a blonde——" Having made this triumphant deduction Mrs. Abrahams drew aside a heavy brocade curtain, and negligently knocked a couple of dozen hat boxes on to the floor. From the pile she selected three.

"You are interested in women, perhaps," said Mrs. Abrahams. This sounded more promising.

"Ah, yes. Yes, why certainly."

It was at times like this that McCann regretted that he was clean-shaven. It was definitely a moustache-twirling moment.

"I am glad of that," said Mrs. Abrahams, "it makes you a more sympathetic customer."

She displayed the first hat, which was of powder blue felt, shaped in a truncated cone and draped with a few careless strands of Heinz Spaghetti.

McCann swallowed hard and asked to see the next.

"Ah, you are discerning," said Mrs. Abrahams, "that was a cheap model. Now this one——"

She revealed a small island of soft fur felt in the middle of a waterfall of feathers and pompoms of duck-egg blue.

Might as well be stung for a sheep as a lamb, thought McCann. "No, I don't like that," he said boldly.

Mrs. Abrahams positively beamed.

"Ah, you are a connoisseur," she cried. "You save the best till the last."

With loving care she parted the tissue-paper and revealed the third of her trophies.

This was a startlingly simple hat of the colour of a very old brown sherry, adorned with a single minute gold feather.

Well, anyway, said McCann to himself ingenuously, a simple little thing like that can't cost too much.

"I'll take it," he said. "I think it should be—er—very suitable. How much is it?"

"You are a lucky young man," said Mrs. Abrahams, with that genuine fervour which is the essence of all true salesmanship, "to find such a hat at such a price. Fifteen guineas."

McCann clutched the counter for support, and at last

succeeded in saying: "That's a little more than I had—er—anticipated."

"If you haven't got the money on you," said Mrs. Abrahams, giving him a shrewd look, "a cheque will do instead."

McCann was feeling for his cheque-book when he saw the warning light. Since coming to the Market he had gone under the name of Melluish—and under this name had registered at the Leopard. His bank, however, was not in on the secret and would be a trifle surprised, to say the least of it, to receive cheques signed by *nom de plume.*

"I think I can manage in notes," he said at last.

"That's all right, then," said Mrs. Abrahams smoothly, as she continued to swathe and tie his purchase.

Having paid his money, McCann felt that he should at least make one attempt at leading the conversation in the desired direction. Putting on a nauseating smirk, which sat ill on his angular Scots countenance, he said: "I suppose you get a lot of pretty girls in here, eh?"

The question was answered from an unexpected quarter.

"Really," said a voice behind him, "the things some men will say."

Turning, he saw the young man whom Sergeant Dalgetty had so unceremoniously ejected from the public bar of the Leopard the night before.

"Ah, Ronnie," said Mrs. Abrahams, "how are you, dear boy?"

"Rapturous," said Ronnie. "I see you are entertaining a celebrity."

Both Mrs. Abrahams and McCann looked a bit blank at this.

"What!" cried Ronnie. "You didn't know. Why, it's all over the Market. This is the famous author who's stay-

159

ing with Kitty Carter at the Leopard, Mr. Melluish."

"Well, there now, Mr. Melluish," said Mrs. Abrahams graciously, "I'd no idea you were an author. Don't go putting *me* in your next book," she added hopefully.

McCann had been doing some rapid thinking. He could guess whom he had to thank for his new role— not a bad idea, at that. More than one author had come to live in the area and, indeed, a whimsical novel by one of them (*The Little Shepherdess of Shepherd's Market*) had recently appeared and had some success.

"I should have described myself as a journalist more than an author," he said.

"Oh, you're too modest," cried Ronnie ("cried" is the nearest one can get to his high-pitched and rather bilious coo). "I expect you really write wicked, wicked books and make heaps of money."

"Well, I must be going," said McCann hastily. "Thank you for the hat, Mrs. Abrahams."

As he left he saw Ronnie lean across the counter and say something to the Jewess. He may have been mistaken, but he thought they were both smiling.

That evening he presented the hat to Miss Carter, and the only satisfaction which he obtained from the whole unfortunate business was derived from her surprised but genuine appreciation of the gift.

"It must have cost the earth," she said.

For once even McCann's modesty did not suffer him to contradict her.

• 2 •

The Reconnaissance of the Atomic Club did not get back until the early hours of the morning, and its members were found, when they did return, to be in no fit state to be cross-examined.

Accordingly it was the next morning before Sergeant Dalgetty presented his report. Glasgow was not present, being still in bed.

"It's some place," he said. "Distinctly hot, sir. That five pound you gave me—it hardly seemed to go anywhere."

It struck McCann that private detection was a more expensive hobby than he had imagined.

"Did you have any difficulty over getting in?" he asked.

"Easy as kiss your hand, sir, what with Miss McDuff to do the talking and me handing out the money. The chap on the door seemed to know her, all right, and she seemed to know him too. He said, 'And who's your friend, Glasgow?' She said, 'Miss McDuff to you, and this is the Archbishop of Canterbury.' 'Can't be,' said the man, 'he's inside already.' After which sparkling piece of repartee I paid out a guinea for each of us— that made us members, for this life and the next—and in we went. Well, sir, it's small, but, as I said, pretty hot. Plenty of anything you may care to pay for. Good food—and drink, and a nigger band. There was a film show downstairs if you cared for that sort of thing. I can't say I fancied it. I'm a simple sort of a chap; I like wine and women and plenty of them and everything the right way up."

"I see," said McCann. "I thought it might be that sort of place."

"Anyhow, the liquor was good. Pre-war Scotch and plenty of it at five pounds a bottle."

"Well, that's reasonable enough," said McCann. "You can pay more than that without going to a night club for it. Apart from the side-shows, which I gather you didn't patronise, did you see anything suspicious?"

161

"Nothing to lay hold of," said Dalgetty. "Just a general nasty atmosphere."

"Did you meet the manager?"

"Manageress—respectable-looking little party."

"Let's have an honest opinion," said McCann. "Do you think that it's worth a further look? Was there *anything* to suggest that it might be the sort of place we're looking for?"

"The headquarters of the gang?"

"Yes—or a meeting-place."

Dalgetty considered for some time before answering.

"It's hard to put a finger on it," he said at last, "but there was, as you might say, a faint stink about the place."

"Can't you be more definite than that?"

"If there *was* anything wrong, sir, it must have been upstairs. I managed to move round most of the ground floor and basement and Glasgow had a dekko at the other parts, and we neither of us saw anything suspicious. There were one or two people who seemed to come and go and it wasn't easy to see where they went to—one large foreign type, in particular. I noticed him because he was alone—didn't bring a skirt with him, I mean, or pick one up off the cab-rank."

"A foreigner? What nationality?"

"Might have been a Spaniard," said Dalgetty, cautiously.

"I see, and he kept disappearing upstairs?"

"I couldn't say that. All I'm saying is, I lost sight of him now and then, and just for curiosity, I looked round a bit, but I couldn't find him, see? Then later, he turned up again, that's all."

"I think I'll go and have a look for myself," said McCann.

• 3 •

Eventually McCann decided to go alone.

Miss Carter asked for a day or two to "fix it", and during that time he lived a life of ignoble ease, doing nothing, very happily, by day, and playing darts with Sergeant Dalgetty during the evening. On Friday evening Miss Carter put on what she described as her "demi-monde" and disappeared, returning at four in the morning, battered but still definitely sober. The next day at breakfast she presented McCann with a visiting card. A pencilled note on the back said: "This gentleman is an old friend of mine." The name on the front was so well known that he could not help eyeing Miss Carter with a new respect.

"That's all right," she said cheerfully. "Just show it to the doorman and you'll have no bother at all. Go tonight—it's Saturday, and there'll be a good crush."

Accordingly, at ten o'clock that evening, having shaken the moth-balls out of his tail-coat and forced his unaccustomed fingers to the construction of a white bow, he presented himself at the entrance of the Atomic Club, armed with Miss Carter's visiting card. Experiencing no difficulty beyond the payment of a guinea, "Mr. Melluish" became a life member of that institution.

His first impressions were distinctly favourable. The house, he guessed, might have been built by some merchant of the eighteenth century. On the ground floor was the huge front room which had served as shop and store, and behind it the counting house. These two rooms between them constituted the whole of this floor. The party wall had been removed, and this made a small but rather charming ballroom. Downstairs, he guessed, there would be the usual cellars, and in the three upper storeys the living-rooms, office rooms and sleeping rooms of the old merchant and his family. Higher up still, probably, the garrets and attics where the apprentices had slept and shivered.

As McCann handed his coat to the girl he made a quick survey. The buffet and bar, later additions to the building, both lay on his right; the swing doors leading to the dance room were on the left. At the far end of the vestibule he thought he saw curtains, and, through them, a glimpse of stairs.

As he was watching them, they swung open and a small woman came down the hall towards him. She reminded him instantly of one of Walt Disney's prissy little rabbits. She had the same twitching nose, the same buck-teeth, the same ineffable air of gaily getting her own way. She advanced on McCann, who decided that attack was the safest course.

"Mrs. Purcell? So pleased to make your acquaintance. Mr. Hinka" (he mumbled the sacred name pretentiously and produced the card) "told me that I must look you up. He said you'd give me a good time."

"The dear man," said Mrs. Purcell. "Any friend of his is a friend of mine. You must consider our little place entirely at your disposal. Entirely."

She tittered, in a way which McCann found distinctly objectionable.

"What would you like to do now?" she went on.

"Well," said McCann. "I'm afraid I've come alone. Do you think you could find me a really *nice* dancing partner?"

"Of course, Mr. Melluish." She pattered ahead of him into the ballroom, which was already more than half full, and led the way to an alcove at the far end, beside the band.

In it were seated half a dozen girls.

McCann gave them a careful once-over, and indicated the youngest and freshest-looking.

Mrs. Purcell tittered again.

"Yes, yes," she said. "I'm sure you'll have lots of fun." She trotted off.

McCann and the girl, who introduced herself as Mavis, retired to a table in a dimly shaded alcove, and did a bit of very respectable drinking. As Dalgetty had said, the whisky was five pounds a bottle and good. The liquor seemed to have no effect at all on Mavis, who was drinking level, or if anything, slightly ahead of him.

She was not a chatty type, and the few words she did volunteer were uttered in a husky, rather attractive voice, which is Life all over, thought McCann. Most girls have voices like metal-saws and never stop talking.

"Would you like to dance?" she asked.

"Not yet," said McCann.

From where he was seated he had an excellent view of the whole room and he examined every newcomer carefully as a possible candidate for the role of Chief Gangster.

They were the usual collection of rather disastrous people who do frequent such places. The bored eyes, the loose lips, the hands that could not keep still. He felt absolutely certain that his quarry was not among them and was at a loss, for a moment, to account for such a certainty; then he realised that they were none of them of the right calibre. The man he sought, whatever his faults, was a *big* man.

There was also the curious certainty, at the back of his mind, that he had seen his quarry before, somewhere, at some time; and that if he saw him again he would recognise him. Certainly he recognised no one in the room at that moment.

He was aware that Mavis was repeating something.

165

"I said, would you like to see some films?"

"I suppose so," he said, and thought that she looked at him rather curiously.

He had noticed for some time that couples were disappearing through a little door at the side of the band platform, and was not surprised when Mavis steered him towards it.

Even thick carpeting and a gilt handrail could not disguise that fact that they were simply descending some ordinary cellar steps. At the bottom McCann was relieved of a further guinea for himself and the girl by a bored plug-ugly who showed them to a sort of small private box not unlike those in vogue in foreign News Theatres.

McCann endured one reel of the epic then occupying the screen—a certain rain-sodden ugliness which suggested that it had come from pre-war Germany—and then, whispering to Mavis that he would be back in a second, he groped his way to the cellar door and found himself once more crossing the ballroom.

The crowd was thicker than ever, and the band was getting into its stride. Mrs. Purcell appeared to be entertaining a noisy all-female party at the far end of the room, and none of the staff was visible—probably all in the buffet or bar, thought McCann.

He walked boldly to the end of the vestibule, pushed through the heavy curtains, and started upstairs.

The first thing which struck him was the complete silence.

At the turn in the stairs the noise behind him ceased as if it had been cut off with a knife.

The corridor in which he found himself was discreetly carpeted and McCann moved quietly along it, listening to the bumping of his own heart.

"Don't be a fool," he said to himself. "They can't eat you. Remember, you're looking for the lavatory. And if anyone comes along, you're slightly drunk."

The doors were all numbered, odd on the right, even on the left, and a quick look into one of them convinced him that they were private dining-rooms. Judging from the complete silence, they were none of them in use.

It was clearly no use wasting time on this floor. McCann made his way up a further flight of stairs and again paused to listen.

The corridor was a duplicate of the one he had left, and yet, somehow, different. It had a more lived-in air, and as he stepped into it McCann thought he heard a voice speaking from one of the rooms at the far end.

He again stopped to listen, but the silence was now complete.

Feeling a desperate distaste for the business, he opened the first door on the left, slipped inside, and feeling behind him, turned the key in the lock. It was a woman's bedroom, and was empty and in darkness. Probably Mrs. Purcell's room. He thought he recognised the saturated floral scent which that ageing primrose had carried with her. There was clearly nothing for him here, and he was on the point of departure when a rather curious thing happened. The Atomic's neon sign, which was of the "one-on and two-off" variety, sprang into life outside, and the back-glow, illuminating the room, shone steadily on the dressing-table in the window. From its heavy leather photograph frame a face looked out at McCann.

The sign flicked off, and the room was in darkness once more.

He had a pencil torch in his pocket, and, getting it out, he shone the beam on the photograph. It was a head and shoulders study of a young man in the uniform of the last war. The face was familiar, but he couldn't place it. It seemed, for some reason, important that he should do so.

So intent was he that the footsteps outside took him entirely by surprise. He stood, frozen, without even the power to turn off the torch.

The footsteps had stopped and someone was fumbling the door handle.

The person outside was clearly surprised to find the door locked. There was an indeterminate sound, which might have been made by a man or a woman—and then the footsteps moved off down the passage to the left.

A door opened and shut quietly.

The noise seemed to release McCann from the spell; he turned off his torch, slipped it into his pocket and tiptoed to the door. Outside everything was still again.

As McCann turned the key and eased his bulk out into the passage, he was thinking furiously.

The most plausible explanation was that the person he had heard had been a servant, coming, perhaps, to do something in Mrs. Purcell's room (did people still turn down other people's beds?). It couldn't have been Mrs. Purcell herself. She would have known that she had left her door unlocked, and would have reacted in a very different way.

McCann hesitated for a moment and then went on down the passage.

From the sound of the closing door he judged that the owner of the footsteps had gone into a room on the left—that is to say, on the same side as Mrs. Purcell's room. It would be wiser to confine any further exploration to the doors on the right-hand side. Wiser, thought McCann, the whole business is stark raving lunacy. It only needs someone to come out of any one of these doors and I'm euchred.

There were two further doors on the right-hand side.

The first of these was unlocked and a glance inside showed McCann that the room, a large one, was completely empty, devoid of either furniture or carpet—a fact sufficiently surprising to warrant comment in London in that year of grace.

He shut the door and moved along to the next.

His hand was actually touching the handle when he heard, from inside the room, a loud click, then a voice, reassuringly matter-of-fact, said: "Yes, who is it?"—a pause—"Oh, send him up as soon as he arrives"—someone was evidently speaking on the telephone.

At this moment McCann heard the door behind him opening.

It was a bad moment, and it made it no better when silence once more supervened.

Someone had obviously come out and was standing watching him. This, he supposed, was the moment when he ought to give a drunken hiccough and inquire if "This—hic—was the way to the gentlemen's lavatory." He found it surprisingly difficult to start acting in such cold blood at a moment's notice.

McCann turned his head and saw Ronnie looking at him.

He had no clear idea of what move to expect next, and what did happen surprised him considerably. Ronnie came quietly forward, caught him by the arm, and drew him down the passage. He was obviously desperately anxious not to make any noise. At the head of the stairs he paused to listen for a moment, then nodded to McCann to go ahead. On the half-landing they stopped.

For the first time McCann turned and looked the youth squarely in the face. He was shaken at what he saw—there is something curiously unnerving about plain terror.

"For God's sake," said Ronnie, "get out of here. Get

out of here at once." His voice was a whispered parody of its usually high-pitched pipe. "I don't know where you came from or how you got here, but for God's sake clear out quickly."

Above them a door slammed.

"Now, quick." Ronnie almost pushed him down the stairs. "Don't stop to talk to anybody. I'll settle your bill. Collect your hat and coat and get going."

• 4 •

Outside the wind was blowing half a gale and the rain was scudding in the gusts.

Somewhere a clock struck three. McCann turned up his coat collar and strode along, wondering savagely if all detection left such a filthy taste.

What a glorious evening!

He had crept upstairs, like some bold bad boy at boarding school, had looked into the matron's bedroom, had sniffed timidly at the door of the headmaster's study, and then, to complete the analogy, had been caught by one of the junior staff, and sent back to bed with his tail between his legs.

(Yet he *had* seen something important. Where had he met the original of that photograph? Try to think.)

And that on top of an evening spent drinking and flirting and dancing in that appalling atmosphere.

A slat of wind almost knocked the breath out of his body as he turned the corner by the Leopard.

To his surprise there was a light in the sitting-room window.

Outside the door stood a War Office shooting-brake with its side-lights on and its army driver asleep at the wheel.

13

Sergeant Golightly's Evening Out

Upstairs McCann was surprised to find Miss Carter yawning desperately, entertaining M. Bren and Colonel Hunt.

"Here's some friends of yours, Angus," she said. "Now don't think me rude, but I'm going to bed. Good night everybody. There's some more beer in the sideboard."

Colonel Hunt sprang to his feet and held open the door. M. Bren bowed punctiliously and McCann opened a bottle of beer.

"We go to France," said M. Bren without preamble. "You had better hurry, *mon vieux*."

"Good God," said McCann. "I thought I was going to bed. What odd times you chaps choose to do things. Why the secrecy?"

"There is no question of secrecy," said Colonel Hunt precisely. "We have been waiting for a suitable storm."

"Well, you've got one now all right," said McCann as a ferocious gust came near to fetching the signboard of the Leopard off its hinges.

"Exactly," said the Colonel. "All trans-Channel traffic was suspended this afternoon. The Met. people say that it probably won't be resumed for three or four days."

"Well, that's fine," said McCann, setting comfortably

in his chair and pouring himself a glass of light ale, "that means we can't go."

"*Au contraire*," said M. Bren.

"It's like this," said the Colonel. "An interruption of cross-channel traffic holds up the leave circuit. Trainloads of troops reach the terminal camps at Ostend and Dieppe, but none of them can get any farther. You see what this means?"

"It means a hell of a crush," said McCann, who had had some experience of Army staging camps.

"It means," said the Colonel patiently, "that your soldier smuggler, who normally only stays in the camp for a few hours, will now be immobilised for three or four days *with the stuff on him.*"

"Yes," said McCann, "I do see it really. I'm sorry to be so dense but I've had a trying evening. When do we leave?"

"The train quits Paddington for Plymouth at four o'clock," said M. Bren.

"You've got half an hour to change and pack. Have you got battle-dress here? Good. It's going to be a rough crossing. M. Bren has all instructions for you. One other thing. You'll be dealing with a camp commandant at Dieppe who is a Major. You'd better become a temporary Lieutenant-Colonel. I'll fix the paper work. Have you still got your crowns up on your battle-dress? Good." The Colonel felt in his capacious side pocket. "Here are the pips to put up with them. Sign for them here, please."

McCann signed the illegible tissue-paper which seems to accompany all Service transactions from the issue of a boot-lace to the handing over of a battleship, and was on the point of leaving the room when a thought struck him.

"Something happened to-night," he said, "which I think ought to be reported to Inspector Hazlerigg."

"Telephone," suggested the Colonel.

"No-o——" Really there hardly seemed anything

definite enough to telephone about. "I think I'll put the whole thing in a written report. There's no great urgency about it."

"Write it in the train," said Colonel Hunt. "Give it to the R.T.O. at Plymouth. Mark it S.M. with this code number. It'll reach London by special messenger tomorrow evening."

• 2 •

Sunday afternoon was already far gone. McCann stood beside the youthful commander on the bridge of the destroyer *Gadfly* and watched Dieppe cliff and fort climb out of the tumbling waste of grey sea.

The destroyer was behaving like a demented kitten and M. Bren, who had spent a good deal of time on the train cursing the parsimony of the British Government for failing to provide them with air transport, was now communing with his soul in some dark recess below decks.

"Do you think you'll be able to berth?" shouted McCann.

"Oh, yes, I expect so," said the Commander. "It's wonderful what a lot of punishment these potato-mashers will take without actually breaking up."

His opinion was justified and it was little more than an hour later that they attained the comparative security of the inner basin, behind the old railway bridge. M. Bren was revived with a patent mixture, the ingredients of which were known only to the Commander, and which was referred to respectfully by the rest of the ward-room as "Operation Crossroads".

On the quay a staff car was waiting for them—further evidence of Colonel Hunt's far-reaching hand—and in less than no time they were sitting down to tea with Major Middleton, M.C., a massive Yorkshireman, Comman-

173

dant of the Dieppe base camp, its surrounds and appurtenances.

"I heard from the War House that you were coming," he said. "Have another cup of tea. No? I don't blame you. Filthy stuff—it's the result of having French orderlies. I never yet met a Frenchman who understood the importance of Warming the Pot. Now, if you'd put me in the picture——"

It was obvious from the first that he meant to co-operate, and McCann heaved an inward sigh of relief. Part of the plan which he had mapped out with M. Bren was of an exceedingly ticklish nature, and he was going to need all the help he could get.

"There are two things we want to try and do," he said. "One is to find out who is receiving the stuff this end, the other is to catch some chap bringing the stuff back again into England."

"What stuff?" inquired Major Middleton reasonably.

"I wish to Heaven we knew," said McCann. "That's one of the things we've got to find out."

"Let us approach ourselves to it logically," said M. Bren. "For the sake of clarity we will call the stolen goods which leave England 'exports'. In a similar manner we may call the final result of the foreign transaction 'imports'."

"The 'exports', I take it, are picked up in England by soldiers returning from leave, carried across by them, and handed over to the organisation on this side. Immediately, do you think, Monsieur, or *en route* for Italy, or after they have got back to their units, perhaps?"

"Immediately, I should think," said McCann. "They wouldn't want them to hang on to the stuff a moment longer than is necessary."

"I am of accord," said M. Bren. "There is, I suspect, a receiving agent in Dieppe itself."

"Yes, but look here," said Major Middleton. "That's

not too easy. The chaps may stay here an hour or they may stay a couple of days. It's all according to the tide and the trains."

"Perhaps," said McCann, "if you would explain shortly how the system here works——"

"Certainly. When a boat arrives all leave personnel are disembarked and brought here in trucks."

"Always?"

"Yes—they have to come here for checking and documentation. Then if there's a train ready, they may be driven straight down to the station again and sent off. On the other hand, if there isn't a train, or if there are a lot of people waiting, with priority, then they may have to stop here—not more than a day, usually."

"You see how awkward that makes it," said McCann to M. Bren. "The chap carrying the 'exports' may be hustled straight from the boat to the camp and the camp to the train. He wouldn't have a smell of a chance of contacting an agent in the town."

"Suppose the agent is *not* in the town?"

Major Middleton flushed a little as the implication came home to him.

"You mean that the receiver may be in the camp—on my staff?"

"I am only trying to be logical," said M. Bren practically. "You yourself have told us that all returning leave-men come to the camp for checking. That must take a little time—an hour or more?"

"Yes, at least. They usually have a meal, too."

"That is what I mean. Whilst they are being 'checked', as you say, they do not remain seated in an orderly manner in their automobiles——?"

Major Middleton laughed.

"I'm sorry, Monsieur," he said, "but it shows how little you know about the British other rank, if you imagine that he is capable of remaining seated in an orderly manner for

175

even five minutes. No—they swarm all over the camp—try to scrounge a second issue of N.A.A.F.I., look for friends, and so on."

"Exactly," said M. Bren. "And that, I suggest, is the moment when the 'exports' reach the receiver."

"It's logical, you know," said McCann.

"H'm. It's a startling idea. One of the permanent staff. And yet—how long has this business been going on?"

"At least eight months."

"Yes. Well, that simplifies things in a way." Major Middleton rang the electric bell and said to the office orderly: "Ask Captain Featherstone to come in."

"That's my adjutant," he went on. "Oh, David, sit down a moment. Have some tea—No? I don't blame you. Look here, can you tell me off-hand how many of the permanent staff have been here eight months?"

"None, sir," said Captain Featherstone promptly. "The first batch all went home four months ago. You remember—when group thirty-eight came out. We had a complete change-over. No, I'm wrong. There is one."

"Sergeant Golightly?"

"Exactly, sir."

"And he's the only one?"

"I'm sure of that, sir—after all, you won't find many chaps deferring their release to serve—saving your presence—in a dump like this."

"No—all right, David. Thank you very much."

"Sergeant Golightly," said McCann thoughtfully.

"I remember his case very well," said Major Middleton. "He's the Sergeant Cook, you know. A very capable fellow at his job—those are some of his cakes that you've just been eating. We were all surprised when he deferred—I don't say we weren't relieved, too, for good cooks don't grow on gooseberry bushes. I'm afraid I thought the worst—there was a girl in the offing."

"I see."

"You know how these stories get round the camp. Everyone seemed to know that Sergeant Golightly used to visit a French girl in the rue *Gamboge*. There may have been no more truth in it than any other camp rumour. He certainly spends most of his off-time in the town. I've often given him a lift up the hill on his way back to the camp."

M. Bren said: "I will make some inquiries in the town. You, *mon gars*, if I might suggest, should make the acquaintance of this enterprising cuisinier."

• 3 •

Late the following afternoon Sergeant Golightly set out from the camp for an evening in town. The storm was still troubling the waters of the English Channel, and throwing occasional capfuls of rain, hail, and spray at the drenched grey port. He had therefore wrapped his rotund figure in a cape and encased his short legs in heavy rubber knee boots (both items of equipment had been designed originally by a thoughtful Government department for protection of troops in chemical warfare).

Despite the early hour, most of the cafés were packed; for the storm had trebled the population of the camp and the men had money saved for their precious home-leave.

Ignoring the better-known places, Sergeant Golightly waddled steadily eastwards towards the port. In a side street, he found the little Estaminet de la Couronne as neat, narrow and unpretentious as half a dozen others in the same thoroughfare.

Here the Sergeant was evidently known and appreciated. Though all six of the little tables were occupied, Madame found room for him in the place of honour beside the bar by the simple expedient of ejecting the young couple already in possession. As an even further

177

mark of esteem she sat down beside him and disposed herself to talk.

"You have neglected us of late," she complained.

"Too much work," said the Sergeant. "The camp's very full now—*Beaucoup de soldats—comprenez?*"

"But perfectly," said Madame in her best English. "It is this—storm."

"That's it," said the Sergeant. "Real grasp of the mother tongue, you've got, haven't you? I'm afraid there's not much doing to-day. What with one thing and another we're a bit short of grub—*Manque de manger —comprenez?*"

He slid his hand under his gas cape and passed across to Madame what looked remarkably like a couple of tins of bully-beef.

Madame received them discreetly and swept them into her capacious reticule with neat sleight of hand.

"But perfectly," she said, "when food is short, all must suffer together. To drink?"

"The usual," said Sergeant Golightly.

An hour later, during which period he had said "The usual" six times, Sergeant Golightly drew out a massive watch (G.S. Signallers for the use of—:). Since "the usual" had been, on each occasion, a generous pernod, he found a momentary difficulty in focusing, but at length decided that the time was eight o'clock.

Good—at least another half-hour before he had to move.

He splashed out some soda-water, a good deal of which went into his glass, and setting back in his seat became aware, for the first time, that his table was being shared by a stranger.

"*B'n soir, Monsieur le Sergeant,*" said the stranger affably.

"*Bon soir* to you, and see how you like it then," replied Sergeant Golightly wittily.

178

"I do no understand. You say——?"

"What you don't understand, cock, won't embarrass you."

"You are philosophe?"

"Oo are you callin' soft? Are you aware that you 'ave the singul-i-ar honour of speaking to the leading light-heavy-medium-bantam-feather-weight champion of Great Britain and Northern Ireland?"

"Indeed?"

"Joke," said Sergeant Golightly. "I'm not a boxer. Not really."

"That I can well believe," said the Frenchman. "Will you do me the honour of joining me in a drink?"

"That," replied Sergeant Golightly handsomely, "is an honour I'll do to any man. Be he black, be he white, so long as his money's all right."

"You are poetic," said the Frenchman, and poured out a "fine" for himself and a quadruple pernod for the Sergeant.

Some time passed and Sergeant Golightly again inspected his watch and discovered with considerable alarm that it was five past two.

"Try looking at it the right way up," suggested the Frenchman, whose grasp of colloquial English was improving as the evening went on.

An inspection on this basis showed the Sergeant that the time was twenty-five to nine.

It was high time to be moving.

Being a very experienced drinker he knew that the great thing was to do nothing rashly. He summoned Madame and demanded his "little bit of blotting paper". Madame appeared to understand perfectly and produced a very large double slice of dark bread with a generous piece of rather soapy-looking cheese in the middle.

After disposing of this the Sergeant felt more in control of the situation.

Obviously the first thing to do was to get rid of the frog. He spent a moment or two formulating the sentence which would achieve this in the most tactful manner, and turning back to the table he had kicked-off ambitiously with "*Mille mercis, Monsieur——*" when he realised that he was alone.

The frog had hopped it.

The Sergeant got cautiously to his feet, and found to his satisfaction that he still had an adequate control of his limbs.

The café appeared to be more crowded than ever, the lights brighter, the noises louder and more cheerful.

The contrast outside was almost theatrical. The wind had increased in strength without losing its playfulness, and it alternately screamed in dry rage and threw capfuls of frozen sleet horizontally down the street.

Sergeant Golightly turned up his coat collar and faced the elements unwillingly.

Nevertheless, the shock of the cold and the sting of the rain had the effect of restoring him to a more cautious frame of mind. He was making for the district which lay behind the old port, and at every turn and corner in the road he stopped for a moment to look back.

He might have spared his pains.

He *was* being followed—by the most skillful trackers alive; men trained to an unbelievable pitch of efficiency by four years of street work in the French Resistance.

As he neared his destination the Sergeant dropped any pretence of secrecy. He was numbed by the vicious assaults of the weather, and he was late for his appointment.

The district which he had reached was sordid even by the limited standards of the neighbourhood. His footsteps had ceased to ring on the cobbles and were now padding and slipping over a thick moss of fish-scales, seaweed, and unimaginable debris. The walls were dripping with filth, and bare except for the occasional ghostly tatters of a poster which had been new when the Germans had entered the town in 1940.

The Sergeant stopped at last in a tiny "impasse", the seaward side of which was taken up by the premises of Messieurs Branchet and Colporteur, a ramshackle building whose long doors, cranes and derricks showed it to be a warehouse on the ground-floor level. A line of shuttered windows above might have indicated offices or a dwelling place.

Suddenly a light went up in one of the windows.

The Sergeant cowered in the deep doorway and waited.

Ten seconds later a second light appeared.

The Sergeant felt behind him, and the tiny *porte cochère* yielded to his touch. He stepped through it into the grateful shelter of the warehouse, and, guiding himself by a thread of light, made his way up the shallow wooden steps to the landing, and pushed open the door under which the yellow light was streaming.

It was an ordinary commercial office and appeared to be the first of a chain of similar rooms each opening into the other. The only occupant of the room was a small man who looked up as Golightly came in.

"You are late," he said, in fair English.

"Yus," said the Sergeant. "It was this——storm."

"You've got the stuff?"

"As per usual——" He felt inside the front of his battle-dress blouse and produced a package about the size of an ordinary box of dominoes. "Carter Paterson, that's me. Always prompt, always cheerful."

Beyond a quick scrutiny of the seals, the dwarf did not trouble to examine the box. He produced a packet of notes and said: "You are prompt, we are prompt also. That is how business should be done." He was counting out the notes as he spoke. "Five thousand francs, as agreed. We add twenty per cent for this consignment. This makes a further thousand francs."

"And ten per cent for the tronc," suggested a polite voice from the doorway.

• 4 •

McCann, who viewed the events of the next few minutes from the passage outside the half-open door, was compelled to admit that he had rarely seen anyone move as quickly as the dwarf.

A second before he had had nothing in his hands but the sheaf of bank notes; now his left hand had swept the box off the table into his pocket and his right hand held an automatic pistol.

"Who are you?" he screamed. "Thieves, murderers. . . ."

"Now then, little horror," said one of the men in raincoats. "Put down that gun. We are the police——"

"Police," spat the dwarf. "You are not police. The police I know. I do not recognise you. You are bandits . . ."

As he spoke he was backing towards the door behind him.

For a moment the situation looked awkward. McCann was unarmed. The detectives carried guns, but they were in their pockets. The resistance was unexpected.

The creature reached the door and flung it open.

He got no further. M. Bren stood there, his bulk filling the aperture.

He advanced on the dwarf, who seemed to be paralysed. "So," he said, "you do not recognise the *agents de police, crapaud*. But you recognise me, *hein*? You know Ulysse, little toad? We have met before, *hein*? Two years ago, in Paris, yes? But on that occasion you hop-hop-hopped away and I was too occupied to run after you. But now it is a different history, yes? Also, you should not play

182

with toys like this." He removed the automatic, as he spoke, and dropped it into his pocket. "When handled by the inexperienced, they explode, causing great mortification. The package also, please. Thank you."

The room had been steadily filling with men as he spoke, and the uniforms and dripping capes of two *agents de ville* now appeared in the doorway.

"We will commit it to you," said M. Bren. "Remove it."

He turned to another of the silent figures. "Take six men and search the building. I think it is empty. But detain anyone you find."

The prime cause of all this, Sergeant Golightly, appeared to have been forgotten. He was standing, in apparent stupor, in the corner. His relief at discovering a compatriot in McCann was most affecting.

"Are you an English officer, sir? Thank God for that. You'll look after me, won't you?"

"Yes," said McCann grimly, "I'll look after you. What's in this packet?"

"On my perishing life and soul," said Golightly, "I've carried nearly fifty of them, but I've never once looked inside."

Illogically, McCann believed him.

Under the paper wrapping was a neatly-made white wood box. M. Bren prised open the lid with his knife.

Inside there lay, gleaming, mint-new and tightly packed, two hundred golden sovereigns.

• 5 •

"I've had a talk with Golightly," said McCann to Major Middleton next morning, "and I believe that he has told me the simple truth. Incredible as it may seem, he just *did not know* what he was carrying. The routine was simplicity itself. A soldier on the returning draft would approach him in the cookhouse and say: 'You're the chap who knows the ropes here, aren't you?' Golightly would answer: 'Yes, but I've been here a long time,' and the chap thereupon handed him a package."

"Always the same sort of package?"

"Identically. The same shape, the same weight, and wrapped and sealed in the same way."

"Did he know the men?"

"No—they were almost always different. One or two of them have done it twice. None more than twice."

"Incredible. Are we all incurably dishonest?"

"They say that you can bribe anyone," said McCann, "if you pay enough. I look at it like this. The man coming back from leave was probably hard up anyway. Someone gets hold of him, and promises him twenty pounds for something that's so easy that it can't go wrong. Or so it seems. Just take the box and put it inside your battle-dress. No one ever searches soldiers coming back from leave. When you get to the Camp at Dieppe, give it to the Sergeant-cook. It's money for old rope. Everyone else is doing it. Why not you?"

"Well," said Major Middleton practically, "the proof of the pudding was in the eating. It must have been a good system, because it worked. It's been going on for eight months without a hitch."

"We might catch a few of the carriers now, I suppose, poor beggars. It's really not them we're after at all."

"I've promoted Corporal Sutherland to Sergeant Golightly's place—he's about the same shape, too. If anyone approaches him with the patter and offers him a package he'll know what to do."

"Yes, I think we've got that tied up all right. It's the next step that worries me—there's a touch of illegality about it that I don't quite like."

184

• 6 •

By Tuesday morning the weather had mended and a notice on the boards warned "Draft X" to parade at 1200 hours and "Draft Y" to stand by for a possible move at 2200 hours.

"Draft X" packed happily and "Draft Y" said: "Just our perishing luck, a night crossing."

At 1230 "Draft X", which consisted of about a hundred and twenty men, climbed into six three-tonners and were carried down to the quay. Here they dismounted, formed column of threes, and marched for about four hundred yards along the quay, carrying their baggage, whilst the lorries, now empty, drove beside them. This was such a normal military manœuvre that it caused no comment.

At the end of the quay was a large shed, and the column was directed behind this, turned left, and told to sit down and wait.

The first ten men, who had formed the leading files and were thus on the right-hand end of the line, found themselves fallen out and marched round the corner of the shed, and out of the sight of their comrades.

The older hands began to scratch their heads. This was a variation from the normal, and therefore suspect. How the rumour started no one knew, but it spread with the speed of a prairie-fire, and, as is the way with rumours, it grew in the spreading.

"'Ave you 'eard what they're doing? Those ten blokes wot went orf first. Searching 'em? I'll say they're searching 'em. Stripped to the skin. Yus. There's about fifty coppers—plain clo'es men, beside the customs. What's it all about? Smugglin' or somethin'. 'Eard about Nobby? That gold ring he had off the *signoreena*. 'E'd

185

put it in the middle of a bully-sandwich, in 'is 'aversack ration. Artful, he? But you know what happened—they 'ad a——great magnet. Electromagnet—yus. That hauled it out, quick as a dose of salts."

Ten more men were led off.

The depression deepened among the remaining hundred. Almost all of them were smugglers in a small way—a hundred cigarettes, a Jerry watch, a bottle of Anisette, a phial of dubious scent from Venice or Milan.

Another quarter of an hour passed, and the Embarkation Officer appeared and gave an order. The remaining men were fallen in and marched on board the waiting transport.

Here they found the first twenty victims, and the general amazement grew. Apparently no one had been searched at all.

"Searched!" said an undersized rifleman. "Whatcher talking about. We bin sitting here kicking our——heels waiting for you——s to come on board."

"One more M.F.U.," was the general verdict of the mystified draft.

• 7 •

No sooner had the gang-planks been taken up and the boat warped off than a curious scene was enacted which would have confirmed the soldiery in their opinion of the higher military mind.

A squad of gendarmes, assisted by a number of civilians, and apparently directed by a Lieutenant-Colonel in the British Army, assembled on the spot on which the draft had been so recently seated. Armed with long iron-spiked poles similar to those used by British Park-keepers, they prodded and poked in systematic fashion up and down the whole area. Another squad searched under the edge of the shed against which the rear line had squatted.

Both parties unearthed a number of things, all of which were brought to the Colonel for his inspection; many of them seemed to cause him amusement.

It was the party searching under the shed who made the find. One of them, feeling with his hands along the central line of piles, felt a place where the sand had been recently disturbed.

He brought his trophy to McCann.

It was an ordinary army water-bottle of painted enamel, brand new.

"Full too, by the weight of it," said McCann. He jerked out the cork and upended it. No water came out.

"More and more interesting." He borrowed M. Bren's knife and cut the stitches of the covering felt, removing it carefully. The secret of the bottle was then revealed. The base had been cut away, resoldered, and carefully replaced; the join in the enamel was patent.

Most of the helpers had stopped work and gathered round in an excited crowd.

"It is, perhaps, an infernal machine," suggested Monsieur Bren, grasping the base plate firmly.

The crowd receded.

McCann pulled, M. Bren twisted, the crowd held its breath.

The plate yielded with a jerk, and a twist of wash-leather shot out, falling to the ground.

McCann picked it up and again untwisted it. Inside there lay two of the most beautiful diamond bracelets he had ever seen.

14

The Bitterness of Failure

"Well now, gentlemen," said the Commissioner of Police of the Metropolis, "I think we are in a position to move."

"From our point of view," said Colonel Hunt, "the sooner the better."

"And ours." Chief Inspector Hazlerigg glanced at Inspector Pickup, who nodded.

Seated on the Commissioner's right was a pale grey gentleman, clothed in that suit of self-effacing rectitude which seems to be the uniform of all senior civil servants. He was, in fact, a permanent Under Secretary from the Home Office, and an Important Person.

"I take it," he said, "that such a drastic step is absolutely necessary. We have to consider public opinion, you know."

Fortunately the Commissioner was well used to dealing with permanent under-secretaries.

"I think," he observed, "that I will ask Chief Inspector Hazlerigg to run over his conclusions for us, gentlemen, and you will be able to judge for yourselves what the position really is."

Hazlerigg cleared his throat.

"In my last report, sir, I told you that we had reason

to suspect that the stolen property—the result of those burglaries which we were investigating—was being disposed of abroad. At the time, our chief reason for thinking so was a negative one—in other words, we were unable to believe that if the stuff *was* disposed of in England, we should have had no hint of it. We had very full and very accurate descriptions of most of the jewellery, and I need hardly remind you that micro-photography and other methods of comparative analysis make it difficult for the criminal to dispose of known stolen articles, especially where these consist of precious metal or precious stones. The stolen goods were all of this character, ranging from rings, watches and bracelets to ingots and loose coins. The bulk of the metal was gold, with some commercial platinum, and a little silver. Monsieur Bren of the Paris Sûreté, whose valuable co-operation has been much appreciated——"

Here the under-secretary made a sort of humming noise, presumably to indicate that the appreciation was official.

"——Monsieur Bren has been in charge of this side of the investigation. By a process of elimination he was able to convince us that the route by which the goods left the country and the proceeds were brought back, was the leave and demobilisation route from Milan, in Italy, through Switzerland, to Ostend and Dieppe, and so across the Channel.

"Our first notion was simply that the goods were disposed of abroad. After examination, however, we discarded the idea. I'm not suggesting that a ready market could not be found for valuables abroad, but the real difficulty was that payment for them would then have been made in foreign currency—Italian, German or French. This would have presented no obstacle if the gang had been operating from one of those countries, but we were convinced that this was not so. We knew, with practical certainty, that the overall direction was English, and the eventual pay-off was taking place in England, and therefore in English money.

"I won't bother you with a summary of the arguments bearing on this point, because they are now out of date. We have, I think, discovered the correct *modus operandi* of the group—thanks largely to the efforts of Monsieur Bren and an army liaison officer who was working with him.

"The system is really very simple. The principal object of the burglaries was to obtain gold. Gold or gold alloy. These metals were used here, in England, for the making of *English sovereigns*. It was a unique form of coining since the article which the forgers were producing had probably more gold in it than the standard minted sovereign itself.

"However, as you all know, it is not just the amount of gold in it which gives the sovereign its unique position on the Continent to-day. Its prime value comes, of course, from its negotiability and its—well, for want of a better term, I will call it reliability. It is hard to strike an exact figure but I see from the latest reports that a sovereign is worth approximately twenty-five pounds in Amsterdam, rather more in Brussels, and thirty pounds in Rome.

"The agent at Dieppe who handled these sovereigns —he's in the custody of the French police, by the way —tells us that approximately fifty packages, each containing two hundred sovereigns, have been dealt with by him alone. We believe that a similar number may have been carried on the Ostend route.

"In total, gentlemen, this gives the group a purchasing power, on the continental market, of certainly not less than half a million pounds."

McCann, who had obtained a seat at the conference through the good graces of Colonel Hunt, was interested to observe that, for the first time, a flicker of real animation had passed across the well-schooled countenance of the permanent civil servant. His lips seemed to savour the words "a cool half-million".

"Our next efforts were directed to discovering what was being purchased with this money, and it is possible that we have not yet got the full answer. One of the lines, however, has now become tolerably clear. They are purchasing foreign jewellery."

Here the under-secretary was clearly on the point of breaking into coherent speech, but Hazlerigg forestalled him.

"I know what you are going to say," he said. "Why go to such absurdly roundabout lengths? Why steal jewellery in England, turn it into cash, smuggle the cash abroad, purchase more jewellery, and smuggle it back into England?"

Since this was precisely what the under-secretary had been going to say, he contented himself with a dignified cough.

"The point is this," went on Hazlerigg. "Having all this money at their disposal the gang was able to purchase not only jewellery, but also the integrity of the jewellery-owner. There was one market above all others which lay wide open to them. The rich and noble of the pre-war period. Men and women whose nobleness was becoming a little part-worn and who were not nearly as rich as they had formerly been. French 'ducs' and 'comtes' whose conduct during the German occupation had been, to say the least of it, not entirely above suspicion—as Monsieur Bren will tell you, there were quite a number of those."

"Of a certainty," said M. Bren. He added a couple of descriptive epithets which fortunately were outside the school-French vocabularies of those present.

"Italian 'marchesas' and 'contessas', most of whose

191

wealth lay now in family jewellery, carefully hidden, first from the German army and then, I am afraid, from the British and American armies as well. People who were anxious to sell, but deeply mistrustful of the currencies of their own country. People, in short, who would sell only for gold, and above all for gold in the supremely negotiable form of English sovereigns.

"You will see how the system worked if I mention one case which came to our notice. The organisation, by an agent, approached the Contessa di Alto-Cavallo and made a round offer of two thousand sovereigns for the best of her jewellery, including the Prebendini family rubies. The offer was, in itself, an attractive one being equivalent, in Italian currency, to about sixty thousand pounds. But they offered her an additional five hundred sovereigns for a statement sworn before a notary that the jewels had been lodged in England *before the war*. This statement also established that the present beneficial owner of the jewels was an English subject. This removed the last obstacle to their open sale in the English market."

"Wait a minute," said the Commissioner. He turned to the man on his left and said: "Can we take it, Sir Charles, that that represents the law on the subject?"

Sir Charles Bladderwick was one of the legal advisers to the Home Office and not to be rushed.

"That would depend," he said, "on the weight given by our courts to a document sworn before a foreign notary. Without going too deeply into International Law——"

"Quite so," said the Commissioner, "but supposing the matter never came into court at all?"

"*If* it appeared that the chattels in question were in England at the date of Italy's entry into the war, and *if* it appeared that they were in the beneficial possession of an English national, and *provided* that there was no

192

question of the bona fides of the transaction, then I do not think that the Administrator of Enemy Property would be able to move——"

"In short," said the Commissioner, who knew Sir Charles fairly well, "you agree. That's splendid. On you go, Inspector."

"There's not much to add," said Hazlerigg. "The result of the manoeuvre was just this. The gang had obtained the benefit of being able to sell their stuff on the open market instead of having to peddle it through crooked dealers.

"The difference in the prices which they could now command was beyond estimation. For example, a diamond ring of a pre-war value of a thousand pounds would fetch a hundred to a hundred and fifty pounds from a fence—a receiver of stolen goods—perhaps a little more. Sold openly, in the present market—which is a 'buyer's market' for all forms of precious stones—well, it might make two thousand pounds. I know that they got twenty thousand pounds for the Prebendini rubies alone. There's no secret about the matter—I was present when they were auctioned at Duke's last month."

"Thank you," said the Commissioner. "I wanted you to hear all that," he went on, turning to the Home Office representative, "so that you could appreciate our difficulties."

"That last point," said the permanent under-secretary, "the importation of well-known foreign jewels—I suppose you're ab-so-lutely sure of your facts?"

"Yesterday," said Hazlerigg, "we intercepted a package of jewellery—no, we didn't catch the carrier, we bluffed him into dumping the stuff and then we picked it up. A pair of diamond bracelets made identification easy; you see, they were more than famous—they were historic. They once belonged to Marie Antoinette."

"Good God," said Sir Charles, "then they must be the property of the Duc de——"

"Exactly."

"It amounts to this," said the Commissioner. "Once the stuff's safely in this country, our hands are tied."

"Can't you have the men who carry it watched?" suggested the permanent under-secretary.

Hazlerigg said patiently: "We've no idea who does carry it, sir. Different men almost every time."

Colonel Hunt spoke apologetically.

"Please don't imagine," he said, "that they have corrupted the entire British Army. We think that fifty or sixty men are involved. Many of them would no doubt draw the line at smuggling drugs or even currency. But the matter is put to them in a most sympathetic light. They are shown the jewels which they have to carry and are told that they are helping out some noble but impoverished family—which of course is more or less true."

"Add to that," said Hazlerigg, "that the risk is negligible and the pay is high."

"I can quite see how it was *worked*," said the under-secretary. "Frankly, it's your suggestion for dealing with it that alarms me. The country's in a very unsettled state about government interference. Couldn't you achieve your objects by increased strictness at the Customs?"

"Impossible," said the Commissioner. "These people aren't amateurs. Those bracelets which the Chief Inspector has mentioned—they were hidden in a specially contrived cache in the bottom of an army issue waterbottle. I've got the thing here. A most ingenious piece of work. What chance do you think a Customs officer would have with stuff hidden like that, and leave men passing through his hands at the rate of five hundred a day? No. I'm afraid this is the only way."

"I'll talk about it to the Minister," said the under-secretary unhappily.

"Passed to you," murmured McCann.

• 2 •

That was Wednesday.

On Friday the storm broke. The early editions of the midday papers had it in the stop press; the later editions gave it the full front page.

GREAT MEDLOC HOLD-UP
FRENCH AND ENGLISH POLICE, C.M.P.s, IN SMUGGLING DRIVE

At nine o'clock this morning every train on the Medloc route from Milan to Dieppe and Ostend was halted and boarded by the police. The raid was carried out by the French police assisted by the regular C.M.P. force, strengthened by C.I.D. operatives and a special team of English, French and Italian customs officials.

Early reports speak of the extraordinary thoroughness and severity of the search. All the trains were taken off the main line and driven into sidings and at the time of writing they have not yet been allowed to proceed.

It is now confirmed that only the home-coming traffic is affected. Nine trains are involved, and an official estimate places the number of men in them at nearly three thousand.

No official reason has been given for this drastic step. . . . Liberties of the Individual. . . . Gestapo Tactics. . . . Slaves or Freemen? (See Editorial Comment.)

McCann read out the paragraph to Miss Carter.

"Even if they find nothing at all," he said, "it ought to frighten the soldiers who carry the stuff. I don't suppose they'll get many volunteers after a show-down on this scale." As he spoke the telephone bell rang.

"Scotland Yard here," said an impersonal voice. "Is that Major McCann? An urgent conference. At once, sir, if you please."

• 3 •

At nine o'clock on that same Friday morning disturbing things happened at the premises of Mr. Leopold Goffstein, Furrier, of Flaxman Street and Berkeley Square. The office was a modest one, consisting of two rooms; an outer one in which Miss Purvis, the secretary, pounded her typewriter, and an inner sanctum, in which, presumably, Mr. Goffstein pondered on the mysteries of the fur trade. Miss Purvis was already seated at her desk, powdering her nose in preparation for the day's toil, when the door bell rang. "See who it is, Sam," she commanded languidly.

The infant Samuel scuttled across the room and opened the door. A small thickset man stood outside.

"Leopold at home?" he inquired cheerfully.

"Mr. Goffstein's not here now..." began Samuel.

"Who is it?" said Miss Purvis plaintively. "What does he want, Sam?"

"It's the police, miss," said Inspector Pickup pleasantly. "And I expect we shall probably want you——" Samuel goggled, first at the detective and then at the two uniformed policemen who seemed to fill the small office; Miss Purvis was too flabbergasted to do more than sit and stare.

"Now—what's that you say about Goffstein?"

"Oh, that's quite right," cried Miss Purvis. "If it's Mr. Goffstein you want, sir, I'm afraid we can't help you. I mean, I would help you if we could, but I can't. He left last week."

"What d'you mean, 'left'?" said Pickup severely. "This is his office, isn't it? That's his name on the door."

"Oh yes, Inspector. It's his name—but it's not his office. You see, he sold the business at the beginning of last week—that was to Mr. Jacoby—Mr. Constantine Jacoby. Then he stayed behind for a few days (Mr. Goffstein, I mean) to show Mr. Jacoby how to run things, and last Saturday he went away."

"Where's Jacoby?"

"Oh, he isn't here either. I believe he has a number of fur businesses like this. He comes down here sometimes to collect letters, most mostly we hear from him by telephone. He'll probably ring up some time this morning."

"I see," said Inspector Pickup. As, indeed, he did. "I suppose Mr. Goffstein left no forwarding address? No. And Mr. Jacoby, he comes here, but you haven't got an address for letters—he just comes here and picks them up? Quite so. And he telephones you, but you don't telephone him. In fact, you've looked through your telephone book but you couldn't find anyone of that name and initials. Strange. Have you the key of the inner door? Thank you, don't bother. We'll manage for ourselves. And Miss Purvis—I must ask you not to leave the office without my permission. You or the boy. That's right. You sit down and have a good cry."

"Speaking from Goffstein's office, sir," said Inspector Pickup. "The bird's flown. He pulled out last Saturday, lock, stock and barrel. Transferred the business to a stooge. Yes, I shouldn't think there's a paper left in the place—except genuine business stuff. I'll have it sorted, of course. And I'm holding the two people here—a woman and a boy. I don't suppose they know anything, though."

Hazlerigg's voice came thinly over the line: ". . . any sign of a wire?"

"I was coming to that, sir. This desk is pretty dusty—I shouldn't think it's been touched for a week. I can see marks on the right of the blotting pad—might easily have been made by a second telephone. Then there's a long, light mark in the paintwork on the top of the wainscoting, and a hole in the floor-boards beside the window. I think that's what we want."

"I see. That's very good."

Hazlerigg's voice sounded cheerful, though a situation was, in fact, developing which might have tried any man's nerve. In front of him, at the Yard, the teletype reports from France were piling up. And they all spelt one word.

Failure.

Plenty of cameras, bottles of spirits, a few illegal firearms, Lugers, Walthers and Birettas, probably battle souvenirs. Considerable surprise and resentment amongst the troops concerned. One contingent had staged a sit-down strike and were refusing to re-entrain.

Five minutes before, he had listened to M. Bren on the cross-Channel line. The Frenchman had been most definite.

"There's nothing here," he said. "I myself assure you."

"All right," said Hazlerigg. "Play the hand out. No apologies and no retractions. I recommend disciplinary action where firearms have been discovered. That's up to the military. Smuggling offences will have to be paid for."

The significance of the failure, however, was startling. If the conveyor belt was empty, then it was a fair assumption that the factory was closing down.

Temporarily—or finally? That was the urgent question.

Pickup's news was another straw in the wind. It was possible, of course, that Goffstein had simply moved hs headquarters. That would be consistent with the known habits of the gang.

But there was a second, less comfortable, explanation. In front of him on the desk lay McCann's last report. This now assumed an added significance.

Yes—he would have to be quick.

He was aware that Pickup was waiting for instructions.

"Leave one man to search the office," he said. "I want you to raid the Atomic Club—get Divisional help. Take enough men to do the job thoroughly. Pay particular attention to the rooms on the second floor—and hold anyone up there who doesn't seem to have any obvious connection with the Club itself. I'll send a Post Office man to meet you. I think you'll find there's a line connection between the Atomic and Goffstein's office. Bring away any black-market booze or other stuff. From what I hear there's enough to send them all down. The proprietress is a Mrs. Purcell. Now listen. I don't want her held. Frighten her; let her go, and have her followed. I shall be standing by here until this thing breaks."

To McCann, when he arrived, Hazlerigg said without preamble:

"I've been re-reading this report on your activities at the Atomic Club. You mention a man who met you on the second floor landing and warned you off the premises. You don't give him a name. Did you know his name, by any chance?"

"No, I only met him on those two occasions—as you were—three occasions. At the Club, at that hat-shop, and I remember him getting chucked out of the Leopard one night. I gather he was quite a well-known local character—youngish, fair haired, rather a pansy type. Everyone called him 'Ronnie', but I don't suppose it was his real name."

"I'm afraid you're wrong," said Hazlerigg. "It's my guess that it *was* his real name. Sergeant Ronald Catlin. He's been working that area under cover for years. One of our 'ghosts'."

"*Sergeant Catlin!* God above. Ronnie was a detective sergeant! You're surely joking——"

"I don't feel very humorous," said Hazlerigg flatly. "Sergeant Catlin has vanished, and—well, I can't help remembering what happened to Sergeant Pollock."

"Silly of me," said McCann. "Stupid thing to say. He fooled me completely, of course. Acted the part to the life. What do you suppose has happened? Do you think they can have tumbled to him?"

"It's no use blinking the facts," said Hazlerigg. "You may have been the last man to see him alive—that Saturday night at the Atomic Club. His reports used to reach us twice a week by a roundabout route. The last time we heard from him was on Friday. The message was 'Sally'. We have a little code for these routine messages. 'Sally' means, roughly, 'I think I am on the track of something'. Normally he should have sent another message on Tuesday, and, as you can imagine, we were pretty anxious to get it. Sergeant Catlin was not the type to send 'Sally' without good reason for it."

"And nothing happened?"

"Nothing. It's my fault, of course, not yours, but if I'd realised that the man you were talking about in your report had been Sergeant Catlin—well, I think I'd have taken a chance and raided the Atomic Club at once."

"You'll do so now?"

"I'm just waiting to hear the results."

The telephone rang.

"Pickup here, sir. I'm speaking from the Atomic."

"Well?"

"I've done what you said. It's a queer set-up, sir, and no question. The local men are in the Club now. They're going through the permanent staff. Most of them are known characters. Yes, sir. Dean Street and Greek Street types. The proprietress now—she's a funny little piece. Half-way between a rabbit and a rat, if you follow me. She doesn't seem scared—more resentful. I'm putting Miss Robey and Sergeant Farrar on to her."

"Upstairs?"

"There's eight rooms on the second floor. Two belong to the old lady—a bedroom and a sitting-room. Two are empty—look as if they've been empty for some time. Then at the end of the corridor there's three furnished bed-sitting-rooms on the left—now empty, and one big room on the right—furnished as an office. That's empty too. Swept and garnished. But I found the wire——"

"Good."

"The P.O. bloke got on to it and plugged in. You were quite right, sir. It connects with Goffstein's office."

Hazlerigg considered for a moment.

"What's the old lady got to say about it?"

"She says the room was let—to a Mr. William Brown. Yes, strikingly original. Present address unknown, but probably somewhere in London."

"Billy Brown of London Town? Did she say what he used the room for?"

"He was a theatrical agent—people used to come and visit him at odd hours. She thought they were clients. No, she didn't know he had a private telephone line. He seemed quite a respectable man to her. Medium height, medium build, no distinguishing features. Hair neither noticeably light nor noticeably dark. She never had any letters from him. He gave no references. In fact, she won't talk. And I don't think we shall get any further unless we are prepared to caution her—and in view of what you said——"

"I see. Did she mention any other boarders?"

"No—she says the other rooms have been empty for the past month."

"Well, that's a lie, anyway. Sergeant Catlin was using one of them as late as last Saturday."

"Sergeant Catlin, sir!"

"Yes—spring that on her and see if you can make anything out of it. And keep at her. The more rattled she gets the better. Keep plugging—oh, wait a minute."

"Ask him," said McCann, "if he noticed a photograph on Mrs. Purcell's dressing-table. The photograph of a young officer in the uniform of the nineteen-fourteen-to eighteen war."

There was a long silence on the other end, and then Pickup said: "I've been along myself to have a look. If it was there, it's not there now."

"All right," said Hazlerigg, "keep trying."

• 4 •

That afternoon Hazlerigg saw the Commissioner.

"Everything points in the same direction, sir, I'm afraid. They've shut up shop. I don't know whether it's temporary or permanent. I hardly know which to hope."

"What about the people at the top?" said the Commissioner. "We want their scalps, you know."

"And I wish I could say that we were close to catching them, sir, but it just wouldn't be true. There are three possible lines—that's all. Mrs. Purcell from the Atomic Club—she's being followed. There's a drag-net out for

202

Leopold Goffstein. And Sergeant Catlin—he may turn up. He's a good man."

But it was failure, all the same. The Commissioner didn't say so, but Hazlerigg knew it. Even McCann knew it. He said to Miss Carter that evening:

"The racket's busted all right, Kitty. I mean, we know how it works, and we can take steps to see it doesn't happen again. But unless we catch the bosses—well, I reckon we're well down on the rubber."

"What'll happen to Hazlerigg?" asked Miss Carter.

"I expect they'll promote him—to a nice innocuous Chief Constableship."

McCann slept badly that night.

15
A Room Without a View

The next morning was beautiful. A blue sky, a soft wind and a candid sun. The first real spring day in the first spring of Peace.

McCann strolled slowly among the crowd of Saturday morning shoppers. Half of his mind was playing with the uncomfortable problems of the previous day, worrying at them in a fitful, useless sort of way, like a sufferer worrying a jagged tooth, whilst the other half was considering, not for the first time, the incongruities of the celebrated Mayfair street in which he found himself, the cheap and hideous upper storeys and the bright, modern and quite disastrously expensive little shops underneath them.

On McCann's left was a celebrated hostelry, and since it was now the proper and legal hour, he turned into it.

Almost to collide with a man coming out.

"I beg your pardon, sir," said the doorman curiously. "Can I do anything for you?"

McCann wondered, with a start, how long he had been standing rooted to the spot, frozen, gaping like a ninny.

"Should I call you a cab, sir?"

"Yes—no," said McCann. "Who was that gentleman? The one who went out just now; I almost ran into him."

He indicated a well-dressed, middle-aged man, by now some ten yards away up the street.

"I'm afraid I can't help you, sir," said the doorman. "He's been in here once or twice, that I do know. Why don't you run after him—you could catch him quite easy?"

"Thank you," said McCann. "Yes, I will."

He turned up the street.

He was still trying to adjust himself to the new situation.

Everything was now so dazzlingly plain. Every problem which had puzzled him the night before was resolved. The man he had just encountered, and was even now following, was the one whom he had seen on that night—how long ago now?—the first night of his leave in England—and in that same hotel. The brick-red skin, the pig eyes, the heavy, masterful chin. It was a remarkable face—and it was the face that had looked at him, for a second time, as he tottered on the brink of unconsciousness in the attic of the chemist's shop near Kensington. And more than once it had looked at him in his dreams.

Every piece of the jig-saw was falling into place. The first time he had seen him he had thought of him as "The Major", and now he realised that the instinct had been a true one. The man *had* fought in the 1914–18 war. He was the original of the photograph in Mrs. Purcell's bedroom.

He was Number One. He was the Boss.

"What the *hell*," said McCann, "what the *hell* am I going to do?"

Call a policeman? He hadn't a shred of evidence. The man would give a name and address—both false

—and would certainly be allowed to depart unmolested.

Follow him, thought McCann, and take damned good care not to lose him. And somehow, somewhere, you've got to get word to Hazlerigg.

They had crossed the Square now, and were both in Davies Street, moving north.

He doesn't look like a walker, thought McCann. If it wasn't such a lovely day he'd have his car out. As it is, he's going to take a taxi soon. If a taxi comes from behind, I'll hail it first and get hold of it. If it comes in from in front, then I'm probably sunk.

He remembered a story M. Bren had once told him of how the lives of six men had depended on whether a certain Gestapo agent shaved before or after breakfast. The lives and happiness of a good many people might depend on which direction the next taxi came in.

Pat upon the thought came a grinding of gears and a taxi lurched out of Grosvenor Street behind him.

McCann raised his arm. The man he was following half turned on the pavement and waved his stick. The taxi driver apparently made a snap decision and went for the better dressed customer.

With the bitterness of death in his heart McCann watched his quarry climb into the taxi and drive away.

A horn sounded plaintively behind him and he realized that he was standing in the middle of the road.

Spinning round, he saw a taxi radiator six inches from the small of his back.

Miraculously the flag was up.

"Are you for hire?"

"I'm for sale," said the driver, "if only you'll get out of the middle of the (minutely described) road."

"Then follow that other taxi," said McCann. "I'm a police officer."

"Where's y' card?"

206

Happily Hazlerigg had supplied McCann with a piece of Scotland Yard's best headed notepaper "Requesting and requiring... all whom it might concern ... to aid and assist Major A. McCann..."

"No offence, Major," said the driver, a spry middle-aged cockney. "I've got my licence to be careful about, y'see. 'Op in."

The other taxi had disappeared.

"S'll right," said the driver. "I know where he'll be going—jest hold on tight and don't worry."

He executed a left and a right, crossed Oxford Street optimistically on an amber traffic light and sped up James Street. Sure enough, the other taxi was there ahead of them, going fast, heading due north, in the direction of Regent's Park.

When they were half-way round the Outer Circle the next piece fell into place. He thought—

I suppose that Mrs. Purcell—so called—might be his wife—just the sort of mousey little wife a man like that would have. No wonder he thought the Atomic was a safe place to hide his office.

Haverstock Hill. Parkhill Road. Mansfield Road.

McCann caught sight of a railway station and read the name as they flashed past. "Gospel Oak." Of course! That was where Polly had had her little adventure. They must be getting close now.

He felt for his notebook and wrote as well as the jolting of the taxi would permit.

"Chief Inspector Hazlerigg, New Scotland Yard. Come to this rendezvous with all the help you can get. Sally—with knobs on."

Parliament Hill Fields, past the bus terminus and up West Hill.

The taxi ahead took a right turn and disappeared. His own taxi overshot the turning and pulled up.

"It's a dead-end, that is," said the driver. "You don't

wanner go down there, Major. He can't get away now."

"Good," said McCann. "What happens down there?"
A bend in the drive cut off his view.

"Two or three houses," said the driver. "Ritzy types.
Big gardens—and a bit of wood."

McCann took the note he had written and a pound
note—his last one.

"I'm going to take a look round," he said. "Will you
drive back to that telephone kiosk—the one we passed
at the foot of the hill—and get through to Scotland
Yard—dial 0 and ask for that Code number. I've written
it down. Give Chief Inspector Hazlerigg this message.
Explain exactly where you left me—and hurry."

"O.K.," said the driver. "Bring 'em back alive,
Major." He turned his cab in the customary double-
jointed manner and disappeared.

McCann advanced cautiously up the drive and
peered round the corner.

As the taximan had said, there were three houses,
disposed round the semi-circle of gravel which formed
the terminus of the private roadway. They were all big
houses, just sufficiently different in style and detail to
suggest that they had probably been designed by the
same architect, and all fronted by high hedges of laurel.
The three of them shared perhaps two acres of garden.

In front of the left-hand one, and possibly the most
secluded of the three, stood the taxi he had been following. As he watched, the driver came out of the gate and
climbed up, swung his cab in a half circle, and chugged
away.

McCann watched him going with mixed feelings.

There was no sign of life from any of the houses, not
even a plume of smoke from a chimney. The whole
place was quiet and in a curious way lifeless. Highgate
West Hill is not a busy thoroughfare at the best of times,

and the strip of wood effectively cut off all noises from the outer world.

After a little deliberateion McCann climbed the low garden wall and pushed forward cautiously into the laurel thicket, which was head high at this point.

Soon he reached the position he was seeking.

He was still just in sight of the roadway along which Hazlerigg must come and he commanded a fair view of the front and side of the house. One curious thing he noticed. Two of the upper windows were shuttered, and his sharp eyes told him that the shutters were steel.

Five minutes passed.

McCann started to do sums. The taxi-driver would take two minutes to reach the telephone—he might have to wait for it—then Hazlerigg would need a few minutes to organise his force and about ten minutes to reach the spot.

Say fifteen minutes in all. Possibly less. McCann had great faith in the Chief Inspector's ability to move quickly.

Footsteps sounded on the pavement behind him, and out of the corner of his eye he saw the bulk of a man climbing the wall.

"Where's Hazlerigg?" he asked.

"I wouldn't know," said the man, who was now standing close behind him.

McCann looked up.

It was one of the largest, nastiest, toughest-looking Jews he had ever seen in his life.

"We're going to play this quiet, see," said the Jew.

He raised his right hand and stroked McCann gently from the hip down to the knee. The sharp blade in his fingers parted the cloth and barely broke the skin underneath.

"Next time I'll lean on it," said the Jew.

209

McCann stood very still, feeling slightly ridiculous, and extremely frightened.

"Walk forward now, mister. Quiet and friendly. I'll do the talking."

The Jew was standing on his right and McCann could feel the steel of the razor against the bare skin of his side. They crossed the lawn.

The front door was opened when they reached it and they walked in.

Inside the long front room were four people. Sitting on the sofa, smoking, was a dark-haired Latin type—undoubtedly the "dago" of whom Andrews had spoken. With his back propped against one of the bookcases was another man whom McCann had never seen before; though his sister would have recognised him, a large and unlovely creature, referred to by the others as Jock. In the corner he was surprised to see the Demon Child.

His attention, however, was focused on the man who stood in front of the fire. Viewing him for the first time with the eye of knowledge, McCann saw the qualities which he had overlooked before. The shrewd eyes, the masterful jowl, the betraying lips.

No one spoke.

The dago continued polishing his shoes with a silk handkerchief, the Child lit a fresh cigarette, Jock coughed, started to spit and thought better of it. The Jew was helping himself to a drink.

I suppose this silence is part of the technique, thought McCann. Well, that's all right by me. In fact, the longer they keep it up the better. If only Hazlerigg would hurry.

"You're Major McCann?"

"That's right," said McCann. "Whom have I the pleasure of addressing?"

The man considered, and then said: "Brown's the name."

210

"Well, Mr. Brown"—McCann tried to infuse a little righteous indignation into his tone—"perhaps you can tell me who's going to pay for my trousers, and what is the meaning of all this?"

"Why were you following me?" asked Mr. Brown.

He asked the question flatly.

McCann opened his mouth, closed it again, and ended by saying nothing at all.

A crippling blow from behind caught him under the ribs and across the kidney. Looking up from the floor, through the waving mist of pain, he saw the Jew standing over him. Saw the bright glint of steel from the knuckles of his right hand.

Hands picked him up and pushed him into a chair.

"When I ask a question," said Mr. Brown amiably, "I like to have it answered at once. It's one of our rules, you understand."

"Yes," said McCann.

"Now, before I ask you the same question again, I'm going to add another one. What do you think it's worth for you *not* to talk?"

"I don't quite follow you," said McCann. The mists were clearing.

"Let's take a concrete example," said Mr. Brown. "Do you think it's worth—say, the fingers of your right hand?"

"No." McCann had been making up his mind as he sat. "Definitely not. I'm sorry—but I'm talking."

He looked round as he spoke. The disappointment in their eyes was so ludicrous that he nearly laughed. The Child in the corner looked exactly as if a promised sweet had been dashed from his mouth. The dago alone looked bored.

Where was Hazlerigg?

"All right," said Mr. Brown. "Why were you following me?"

"Because I recognized you."

"Explain that, please."

"I don't expect you'll believe this for a moment, but first saw you months ago—at the end of last Novembe at the——Hotel. I didn't know it was you of course. just—er—remarked on your face."

"All right," said Mr. Brown. He seemed imperviou to sneers as to heroics. "Go on."

"Some time after, you may remember, I followed th late but unlamented Blanco White to Kensington. You usual method of receiving visitors seemed to be to h them with a blunt instrument. On that occasion yo excelled yourselves, and I was knocked out twice. Th second time, just as some person was about to come i at the door. Presumably, in fact, I was knocked out s that I should not be able to see who that person was. I didn't quite work. I did see it—it was you."

The person who seemed to take this reminiscenc least well was the Demon Child. No doubt he felt that i reflected on his professional skill. He started to protest intercepted an urbane and thoughtful look from Mr Brown, and desisted.

"At the time," went on McCann, "my idea of th connection between the two occasions was rather misty I knew that I had seen your face before, and I knew tha I should recognise it if I saw it again. This morning saw it again."

Keep quiet about the photograph, thought McCann —it's dynamite. Where the hell is Hazlerigg?

"I see," said Mr. Brown. "Not, as you say, a very likely story. So unlikely, in fact, that it might even be true. One further question. When you saw me and fol- lowed me this morning, were you alone?"

"Yes—quite alone." Stick to the truth if possible.

"And you followed me on your own?"

"Yes—considerably against my better judgment."

"Why do you say that?"

"I wanted to get help," said McCann, with what he hoped was a disarming candour. "You see—I remembered only too clearly what had happened last time I tried to play the hand on my own."

"Then why didn't you get help?"

"There was no time—I saw you in Berkeley Street. You were on foot. I picked up a taxi a minute after you did—in Davies Street—remember? I hadn't time to do anything but keep on your tail."

"Yes?—and afterwards?"

"I don't follow you."

"Surely it occurred to you to send your taxi-driver back with a message for the police."

McCann felt that his mouth was unaccountably dry.

"It *should* have occurred to me," he said, "but believe it or not, it never did."

"Since you offer me the choice," said Mr. Brown, "I *don't* believe you. By the way, I think that this is yours."

He threw down on the table a pound note.

McCann felt sick. For some reason he found himself thinking of Sergeant Pollock, whom he had never met.

"The note to Inspector Hazlerigg," went on Mr. Brown, "I shall retain. It shall join my collection of famous last works." The man was positively purring, bubbling over with pleasure. "Both taxi-drivers were members of our little troupe, of course. That's just a safety play—known in America as the double-taxi convention—invented, I believe, by the redoubtable Dion O'Banion."

McCann tried to force himself to think.

"What are you going to do?" he asked—and was himself surprised at the question. It certainly wasn't what he had intended to say.

"Curiosity," said Mr. Brown gently, "seems to be your besetting sin. Since you ask, I shall probably set you in concrete and add you to the foundations of Waterloo Bridge—you have until to-night to think it over. Any alternative suggestions of an amusing nature which you may put forward will receive our closest attention. Take him up."

McCann staggered to his feet. His hip still hurt abominably. Jock gripped him professionally by the upper part of the left arm. The Jew fell in, two paces behind. In silence they climbed two flights of stairs and went down an uncarpeted passage until they reached the door at the end. This had a square grated hole cut in it, about two-thirds of the way up, and McCann noticed that the Jew took a quick look through this judas before stooping to unlock the door.

"Here's some company for you, Clarence," he said, and at the same moment Jock shifted his grip and thrust McCann sharply forward.

The door clanged shut, and the footsteps died away down the passage.

McCann saw that he was not alone in the room. In the farthest corner, lying on a little pile of army blankets, was "Ronnie".

"Good God," said Ronnie, climbing to his feet. "What are you doing here?"

"I might ask you the same, Sergeant," said McCann.

"You know who I am, then," said Ronnie.

"I do now. I didn't when I met you at the Atomic Club—you remember? What happened?"

"Everything happened. Everything happened at once. I think they suspected me for some time. They nabbed me that night. I've been here for days—weeks."

"It's certainly snug," said McCann. In the relief at finding an ally his spirits were wonderfully restored.

The room, in fact, was bare.

Apart from the pile of blankets on which the Sergeant had been lying there was nothing at all. The windows were shuttered, the walls were of unplastered cement. The electric lights were inset behind thick glass, let into the high ceiling. It looked like a condemned cell.

"Well," said McCann, when he had completed this brief survey. "How do we get out?"

Ronnie laughed mirthlessly.

"That's how I used to think, sir," he said, "for the first few days. You'll soon find out. This room wasn't built to be got out of. Just take a look at those shutters, for a start. Steel shutters and steel bolts. Every bolt locked through on the outside—a lovely job."

"The door?"

"It took me twenty-four hours to shift one of the panels. Look!" He held up his right hand and McCann saw the torn fingers. "Then I found out what I ought to have guessed before. It's steel-lined—on the outside. The lock's on the outside too, of course."

"The floor?"

"I've made no impression on it yet—but you're welcome to try—it's six-inch oak boarding—but please don't mention the ceiling—because we've nothing to stand on—and we're neither of us fifteen feet high—and even if we could reach it the room above us is occupied."

McCann had seated himself with his back to the wall. Now he looked thoughtfully down at the youngster lying beside him—at the white face and the twinkling eyes.

He selected his next question with some care.

"Have these people—hurt you?" he said at last.

Ronnie flushed. "No," he said. "No, sir, they haven't touched me. What made you—I mean, why did you say that?"

"Just this," said McCann equably, "that they seem, somehow, to have got you down. You've managed to convince yourself that the situation's hopeless. You've done nothing but tell me the ways by which we *can't get* out."

"I'm sorry," said Ronnie. "Fact is, perhaps the morale was a bit low. It was being alone and not knowing where I was or how long I'd been here—or what was going to happen next. My watch stopped when I was unconscious—I didn't know if it was night or day—*they never put this light out*, you see."

"Yes, I see." McCann's voice was hearteningly matter of fact. He was Major McCann once more. He was in charge.

"How often do they come round?" he asked.

"About once every two hours."

"Do they come in?"

"Not unless they're bringing me food or letting me out—that happens sometimes—quite good food, too."

"Then the other times—what happens?"

"One of them just comes past the door and looks in."

"Let's get this quite straight," said McCann. "It may be important. At odd times in the day they come up and give you food—and let you out."

"Yes—down the corridor to the lavatory. On those occasions there have always been two of them."

"And this two-hourly visit of inspection—is that made by one man or two?"

"Only one—hold it. Here he comes."

Footsteps sounded along the passage. McCann was aware of eyes regarding him through the grating. It was a careful examination, which took some minutes. Then the footsteps went slowly away. McCann looked at his watch. It was exactly one o'clock.

"The food should be coming along soon," said Ronnie.

"I don't think we shall get any food."

"Oh." Ronnie looked up. He was not exactly scared, McCann decided. But his treatment of the last week—

the efficiency and silence and impersonality of his gaolers—had served to sap his resistance. His courage was still intact, but his will-power was compromised.

"I gather to-day may be our last day."

"I see."

"Have you picked up any ideas as to why they've been waiting here—and what they're waiting for?"

"Yes," said Ronnie. "I think I know that. They closed the organisation last Saturday night. I think they meant to shut down anyway—when they found me smelling round the Atomic they called time at once."

"Then why haven't they disappeared to the four corners of the earth with the proceeds—they could catch the boat-train to-night—for all we could do to stop them," he added bitterly.

"It's not quite as simple as that, sir. Two of them are known. Goffstein—he's in hiding somewhere in this house—there's an 'all-stations' out against him—and that kid, I don't know his name."

"Oh, the Child Menace—yes."

"The others would go if they could, but they haven't got all the money in yet. There were to be three big sales all coming off this week—but one of the lots got lost—some French stones."

"Yes—we got those," said McCann. "I'll tell you about it in a moment. Go on. Are these the final sales?"

"I think they must be," said Ronnie. "Yes, I think they must be."

Final Clearance Sale, thought McCann. Damaged and unwanted stock. Item, one police sergeant the worse for confinement. Item one ex-army Major, last year's model.

Ronnie was talking.

". . . if that's so, sir, we ought to think something out and do it pretty quick."

"I've done all the thinking," said McCann simply. "It

217

wasn't difficult. There only *is* one plan. I'm taking your word for it that we can't break out by ourselves———"

"There's no harm in trying, of course," said Ronnie, "but I think we'll be wasting our time."

"Exactly—then that only leaves one chance. We shall have to rush them when they come to fetch us."

"All right," said Ronnie. "It's not going to be easy. Whenever they came to let me out, one of them looked through the spy hole first—to see that I wasn't lying in wait for them behind the door or any boy-scoutery of that sort. Then he opened the door and came in— while the other stayed outside."

"That's much what I thought," said McCann calmly. "In fact that's just the procedure I'd been banking on. If only two of them come, then we've an outside chance. If they send three—well, we might as well give them a run for their money. Now here's how it goes. We'll split this pile of blankets into two"—McCann suited the action to the words—"and lay out two beds, both against this wall, in full view of the door. It's past one o'clock now—and it doesn't get dark before six. We can expect to be looked at at three o'clock and five o'clock. At both those inspections I want the man to see the identical picture. You will be asleep on your bed—I shall be squatting on mine, with my legs tucked under me, thinking hard about nothing. All right so far?"

"Carry on, chief," said Ronnie. McCann was glad to see the tiny signs of increasing confidence. They were going to need all of it.

"All right. Now we wait for zero hour. And zero hour is the moment when we hear *two or more* people coming down that passage. That's when we're going to need to move quick. What sort of shoes have you got on?"

"Dancing pumps," said Ronnie disgustedly. "Not much use, I'm afraid. Part of the old get-up."

"I wasn't thinking of them as weapons. Look now—

218

we'll roll up some blankets under the bedclothes—I take it you usually sleep with your head under the blanket to shut out the light—just so—and we'll add a touch of verisimiltiude to this otherwise extremely bald, not to say, corny deception by exhibiting your shoes sticking out from under the end of the blankets. Let's try it now."

Half an hour's work produced a passably lifelike figure. It was extraordinarily difficult to arrange the shoes at anything like a natural angle, but they got it at last.

"I'm beginning to get the hang of this," said Ronnie. "I suppose that I hide behind the door."

"Not behind the door. Flat against the wall on the side that it opens. The next thing is—weapons."

Ronnie's face fell. "I'm afraid I've got nothing. They stripped me pretty thoroughly, and, as you can see, there's nothing movable in this room at all—except those blankets. I suppose we might rig up some sort of sandbag."

"I think we can do better than that. First, I'm prepared to sacrifice one of my shoes—see how you like the feel of it."

It was a formidable, iron-studded, thick-soled walking shoe, which must have weighed two pounds.

"Mind you," went on McCann, "I don't like the idea of tangling with these types in bare feet any more than you do—but I see no way out of it."

"What are you going to use?"

"I'll show you." McCann extracted his thin leather wallet, and a handful of coins. "This is the knuckleduster Mark I—rough but effective." He folded the wallet into a fat cylinder and grasped it in his right hand. Then he selected two florins and a half-crown ("milled edges, better than pennies," he said genially) and inserted them, edgeways on, between his clenched fingers.

"The things they teach you in the Commandos," said Ronnie admiringly.

"Commandos!" said McCann. "I learnt that at my prep. school—now let's start rehearsing."

The next three hours were in some ways the most singular McCann had ever spent in his life. What little they could do by way of preparation had been completed. There was nothing else to do but wait.

He himself was physically not uncomfortable. He was sitting on the blankets, his shoeless foot tucked under him, his armed right hand lying under his coat. Experiments had shown that from a sitting start he could reach the door in just under two seconds. After that everything would have to be left to chance. But his mind was desperately perturbed.

At three o'clock and again at five o'clock a face had peered at them through the grating. McCann thought he had recognized the Jew. No word had been said and the door had remained shut.

Ronnie was sitting against the wall now, ready to get into position. His face was very white and it was difficult to say what he was thinking. Attempts at conversation had been given up long since.

The minutes crawled by.

Supposing they don't come at all to-night, he thought. Perhaps Mr. Brown was just pulling my leg— it would be well in keeping with his sadistic soul. God, if I could get my fingers on him once—just once.

"Someone coming sir," said Ronnie. He stood up quickly, and flattened himself. "Only one, I think."

"More than one," said McCann. "Two at least."

His heart was thumping and the blood was hammering in his head.

Normal, you fool, Angus; look normal. Stop scowling. Take a grip of yourself. This is it.

What followed seemed to McCann to happen in the

220

slow motion of a nightmare.

Eyes looked through the grating. There was a mutter of conversation. It was impossible even at that point to say with certainty whether there were two or three men outside.

The lock clicked, the door swung open, and the Scotsman, Jock, stepped quickly into the room.

"Stand well back, and aim for the temple," McCann had said.

The heavy shoe seemed to hover interminably. Then there was a sound such as a leather cricket ball makes as it meets the soft surface of a cricket bat.

Jock crumpled forward.

McCann saw Ronnie drop the shoe and leap quietly through the doorway.

The he found himself on his feet.

He didn't know whether Jock was finished or not, and there was certainly no time to find out.

As the Scotsman tumbled forward, he hit him square in the face.

In the passage some desperate action was obviously going on, but it took McCann a vital second to clear the body of his adversary in the doorway.

Outside, things were not going well. McCann had seen all along that the tiny delay necessary for Ronnie and himself to get through the doorway and into the passage would give the opposition side just enough time to square up to the attack. There was only one man there, but it was the big Jew and he knew the ropes.

Ronnie had simply thrown himself at him and had succeeded in getting his hands round his throat. Nine men out of ten would have wasted time trying to tear those hands away. The Jew was the tenth. Steadying his broad back against the wall he had shifted his weight on to one foot, and then brought down the heel of his other boot hard on to Ronnie's stockinged foot.

221

There was a horrid crunch and a noise, half gasp, half yell, as Ronnie collapsed. As he went down some merciful instinct caused him to maintain his grip on his adversary's throat.

It was at this moment that McCann arrived.

The Jew was bending half forward under Ronnie's sagging weight and his attention was distracted. McCann pivoted on to his left foot and put all his weight and strength and skill into one whole-hearted uppercut.

The Jew buckled to his knees and his head sagged forward. McCann kicked him hard in the throat.

The fight was over.

From beginning to end it had taken almost exactly ten seconds. McCann found himself gasping for breath as if he had run a mile. His right hand was swollen and thick with blood—some of it his own. He noticed that two of the coins were still in place, and slowly picked them out and dropped them into his pocket.

Someone said: "Quick. No time to waste."

He was never quite sure whether it was himself or Ronnie.

Stooping, he grasped the Jew's ankles and dragged him along the passage and into the room. Jock was lying where he had fallen. He went back and, getting an arm round Ronnie, he half carried him back and sat him down against the wall.

"It's no good," said Ronnie, with a very white face. "I can't move. If I put any weight on this foot I shall pass out. For God's sake clear out quick and get help."

"All in good time," said McCann. His mind was working again now.

A rapid search produced one gun—a German automatic with a full clip of nine—a cosh, a pair of steel "knuckles" and the door key. He pulled the two bodies over to where Ronnie was sitting and laid them face downwards on the floor on either side of him.

"Tie their wrists together," he said. "Use their ties and handkerchiefs and belts. Start with Jock. I think the Jew's dead—but don't risk it. Tie him just the same."

"O.K.," said Ronnie, "but hurry."

"I'm just going," said McCann. "Take this—you'll need it." He passed over the gun. "I'm going to lock the door on the outside. There's just a chance that this is the only key. Anyway, if you sit well back you'll be out of range from the spy-hole. Good luck."

Thirty seconds later he was creeping down the stairs.

As he reached the first floor landing he heard steps coming up and Mr. Brown's voice said: "Jock—Benny. What the hell's wrong with everyone to-night."

McCann opened the first door he saw and slipped inside. It was a bedroom, he saw, and mercifully empty.

He waited until he heard the footsteps starting up the second flight to the floor above. It was a fair drop, with what looked, in the dark, like a flower-bed.

He threw one leg over the window-sill, turned on to his stomach, slid out the full length of his arms, and let go. The flower-bed, he discovered, was full of standard rose-bushes.

As he picked his way painfully to his feet he heard a shout from inside the house, high up. And then the slam of an automatic.

16
Finale

The machinery was running at full throttle now. Hazlerigg sat in his room at Scotland Yard and listened to the reports coming in.

Throughout the metropolitan area and out into the fringes of the home counties hundreds of policemen, squad men, uniformed and plain-clothes detectives, searched and patrolled and asked questions—and listened.

They were looking for Leopold Goffstein, late of Flaxman Street, and they had several excellent photographs to assist them. They were looking for Benjamin Kraftstein ("Benny" the Jew had been identified at last). They were looking for a youth "name unknown, aged approximately nineteen years, height five feet nine inches, hair brown, no distinguishing marks"—and all they had to help them in that case was a seven-year-old photograph taken from a boxing group.

They were looking, too, for Sergeant Catlin and Major Angus McCann, the last as the result of a panic-stricken telephone call from Miss Carter which had reached the Yard at four o'clock that afternoon.

"I sat in the North-West Auction Rooms to-day," said

Hazlerigg to Pickup, "and watched the Demarest diamonds being sold by Curliers. I don't think they knew who they were really acting for—I did."

"Couldn't you have stopped the sale?" said Pickup. He knew that he was talking nonsense and the telephone bell saved Hazlerigg from the necessity of answering.

The instrument cackled for nearly a minute.

"No," said Hazlerigg at last. "I'm sorry. Yes, I quite agree. It's not definite enough to act on. Keep him under observation."

"Who's seen who—and where, sir?"

"Goffstein's been seen in Whitechapel."

"And Birmingham and Welshpool and—oh, yes, Saffron Walden."

"He gets about," agreed Hazlerigg.

The phone bell went again.

"A resident of Highgate," said Hazlerigg at last. "Whereabouts?—Oh, the Holly Lodge Estate—yes, wait whilst I get a map, please. Go on. I see. Yes, all right. You can take that up. Report back here."

To Pickup he said: "Highgate police have had a man in who reports hearing revolver shots. He says they sounded like an automatic. He also says that he fought in the Infantry for six years and knows an automatic when he hears one."

"That's not saying it's anything to do with this case, sir, even supposing he's right."

"Of course not," said Hazlerigg. "Go and get some dinner, there's a good chap. I'll have mine when you get back—hold on, here's another."

"Hello—hello. Yes. Who?" Something in the Chief Inspector's voice halted Pickup at the door.

"Oh, well done, Major," said Hazlerigg. "Well done indeed. Yes. Hold on, we're coming."

• 2 •

At the foot of Highgate West Hill, Hazlerigg issued his operation orders. The few citizens who were about at that hour gaped at the concourse of Squad cars which had materialised so softly and now seemed to fill the road. Pickup was talking to the Superintendent from Highgate. He ran across to the Chief Inspector.

"They've got the man here, sir," he said, "—the one who was going to investigate the shooting when your message came through. He says he knows the house well."

"All right," said Hazlerigg. "He can come with us as a guide. One car ahead now, to block the driveway. The rest of you on foot from here."

The Superintendent said: "My men are coming down from the top, Inspector. They ought to be in position in a minute."

"Thank you, sir," said Hazlerigg. "Other cars to follow in three minutes."

The stage emptied.

At the corner of the private roadway was the driver of the Squad car which had gone ahead to block the entrance. He had some disquieting news for them.

"Just a matter of a split second," he said. "As I brought the car over, out he came—on a motor-bike. Missed my bumper by an inch. Turned up the hill."

"Did you recognise him?" asked Hazlerigg.

"Young chap, sir. Slim sort of build—and a white face. That's all I could see. I'd have stopped him if I could, sir——"

"All right," said Hazlerigg, "I'm sure you did your best. The Superintendent's men will probably have picked him up at the top."

226

The Superintendent loomed in front of them.

"We're all round the house now," he said. "Shall I give them the word to close? I'm leaving this part to you."

"Thank you very much, sir," said Hazlerigg politely. "I think I'll give the house a knock first in the routine way."

As he spoke, the clouds which had been thinning for some time shredded away, and the clear cold full moon rode out.

Hazlerigg walked up the path alone. The click of the golden gate as it shut behind him was startlingly loud. His footsteps crunched on the gravel. From the house no gleam of light showed. As far as McCann could make out from his vantage point in the laurel hedge, all the downstairs windows were shuttered.

"It's Lombard Street to a china orange they're all away," he thought. "When Mr. Brown found that I was gone, he must have known—that gave him a clear ten minutes to get cracking—unless he stopped to deal with Sergeant Catlin."

McCann's eyesight, as has been said, was good, particularly at night. He saw the shutter of the front room swinging back and caught the flicker of moonlight on steel.

Three voices shouted at once.

Hazlerigg, whose hand was outstretched to the door, flung himself sideways, rolling as he fell, so quickly that the action seemed to synchronize with the opening of the shutter and the burst of fire.

McCann was deafened by the crack of an automatic from almost behind him and turning his head, he became aware that M. Bren was standing in the edge of the shadows, a gun in either hand.

As he looked the Frenchman fired again. It was good practice, at thirty yards, and at night. Every shot was

227

hitting the steel shutter and the man behind the shutter was clearly afraid to open it further.

Hazlerigg, apparently unhurt, had taken advantage of this diversion to disappear into the line of hedge nearest the house.

"Flip me," said a cheerful voice from behind the wall, "talk about the battle of flipping Sidney Street—this is it."

"Keep yer head down, Nobby. Remember you're only six months orf y' pension."

"Keep those men quiet, Sergeant."

Outside in the road McCann found the Superintendent and Inspector Pickup. A moment later M. Bren joined them.

"They mean business, all right," said the Superintendent. "I hope——No, here comes the Inspector. He looks all right."

"Thanks to Monsieur Bren," said Hazlerigg. He, like McCann, seemed to have encountered a painful number of rose bushes in his escape, and was wiping blood from his cheek.

"I have never understood before," said M. Bren, "why the British policeman does not carry a weapon. Now I comprehend. Had they been armed to-night"—he indicated the line of excited constables behind the wall—"nothing could have saved you."

"What's the next move?" said the Superintendent. "Have to wait for the military, I suppose."

"They won't be long, sir," said Hazlerigg. "I gave Colonel Hunt the word before I started—just in case. And talk of the devil——"

An unmistakable figure had materialised beside them.

"I have a section of the Brigade of Guards in two trucks at the end of the road," said Colonel Hunt. "I heard firing as I came up——"

228

"They fired on the Chief Inspector," said the Superintendent.

"Splendid," said Colonel Hunt, "splendid. That regularises the situation at once. This is Lieutenant Sir William Carpmael, who commands the section. He will have the actual handling of the troops of course."

Lieutenant Sir William Carpmael plucked at his long blond moustache and then said: "Well, now, perhaps you could put me in the picture."

"We shall have to rush the house," said Hazlerigg. "Since none of my men are armed, I propose to keep them well back, as a cordon. Lessen the chance of accidental casualties that way."

"Right," said the Lieutenant. He surveyed the moonlit scene for a long minute and then pointed to the house on their immediate right—the middle one of the three buildings. "What about kicking off from there?"

"Just what I was going to suggest myself," said Hazlerigg. "It will make a good starting-point and it will give us cover up to the last ten yards."

"We'll put the P.I.A.T. there, too," said the Lieutenant. "Sergeant!"

Not the least surprising happening of that surprising evening was that when Hazlerigg, after a cautious approach, rang the bell of the centre house, the door was opened by a smart parlour-maid.

"Excuse me," said the Inspector, "but is your master at home? Don't be alarmed, miss, it's quite all right."

"Yessir," said the girl faintly. Before her startled eyes the hall seemed to be filling with enormous policemen and no less enormous soldiers. "Mister Pilkington—sir. He's in here, sir. Shall I announce you?"

"Now, don't you bother," said Hazlerigg. "I'll announce myself." Six more guardsmen arrived, carrying a P.I.A.T. projector and two Bren guns. The girl retired down the kitchen stairs to have hysterics in the basement.

Inside the room she had indicated Hazlerigg found Mr. Pilkington, a neat, bird-like man of some eighty summers. He looked up from a game of patience, which he was setting out on a small table in front of the fire, and regarded the Inspector with considerable surprise.

The question as to why so far he had shown such a lack of interest in the violent and exciting scenes being enacted around him was in part resolved. He picked up from the table an old-fashioned horn ear trumpet.

He was clearly very deaf.

"Excuse me," bawled Hazlerigg, "but we shall have to make use of your house. Good gracious me—I didn't realise there were quite so many of us."

Before Mr. Pilkington's fascinated eyes, there entered in succession Inspector Pickup, four uniformed policemen, M. Bren (a fearsome figure with two long German automatics belted outside his mackintosh), a Sergeant and six Guardsmen, Lieutenant Sir William Carpmael, Major McCann, Colonel Hunt and, finally, the Highgate Superintendent.

"Would you see if you can explain things to him?" said Hazlerigg optimistically to the Superintendent. "Here, for God's sake, Inspector, take some of those constables back into the hall. I think we'll find what we want through here." He indicated a connecting door which evidently led to the dining-room.

"Keep your heads down, now," said the Lieutenant, "they can see you from that side of the house. Corporal, we'll have the P.I.A.T. at at the middle window. Bren guns on either side. Sergeant, when I turn the light out I want you to get the rest of the men out of the two end windows and into the flower border, lying down."

"Very good, sir."

230

"We'll give you cover if they open up, but no one's to fire until I give the word. Carry on."

He turned the switch and the room was plunged into darkness.

McCann, who was crouching beside M. Bren and the Inspector, viewed the last fantastic act of the night's drama by the light of the full moon filtering in at the three long dining-room windows.

How good the Guards were—always. He noticed that not one of them had said a word about the whole extraordinary business. Absolute silence, absolute discipline. The Lieutenant seemed to know his stuff too.

Outside the dining-room windows was a low herbaceous hedge, and behind this there were now about a dozen Guardsmen lying. Twenty yards away, through the trees, the other house stood silent and shuttered in the moonlight.

McCann was watching the Corporal, who was sitting behind the heavy anti-tank projector at the centre window. The Lieutenant was crouching at his side.

Suddenly, from inside the house they were watching, came the double crack of an automatic.

"What the blazes is that?" said Hazlerigg, quietly. "Have they started shooting each other?"

"It might be Sergeant Catlin—I'm afraid." McCann, too, found himself whispering.

The Lieutenant seemed not to have heard the sound, or if he had, he gave no sign of it, but continued to watch the Corporal who was fiddling delicately with the sights of the projector.

"The middle of the shutters," he said. "Aim for the join."

The Corporal nodded.

The Lieutenant placed his fingers in his ears and everyone in the room hastily did likewise.

The noise of the detonation was curiously soft, followed almost immediately by a shattering roar as the projectile struck the shutters squarely.

The window dissolved in a cloud of yellow smoke. As it cleared, the watchers could see no window at all, but a jagged hole in the brickwork, and through the hole the leading Guardsman was climbing.

The Lieutenant was half-way across the lawn, and behind him, a smile of supreme satisfaction on his face, trotted M. Bren.

McCann got up on to his feet. He felt desperately tired but he knew there was one more job to be done. By the time he reached the house everyone else seemed to have disappeared. A long arm in battle-dress reached out and pulled him through the hole.

Somewhere on the other side of the house, a battle was going on.

McCann ignored it, turned up the stairs and reached the second floor, without meeting a soul. The long corridor was empty, too, and at the far end a square of light showed from the open door of his recent prison.

With a sudden and irrational presentiment he hurried forward. Instinct flattened him at the edge of the doorway and the bullet, fired from inside the room, buried itself in the plaster a foot in front of his nose.

Enlightenment came. "For God's sake, Sergeant," he said, "a little discrimination please. It's me—the Navy's here."

"Thank God for it," said the voice of Sergeant Catlin faintly. "That was my last bullet."

· 3 ·

Downstairs the fight was over. Considering the amount of lead which had been thrown about, there was surprisingly little damage. Two of the soldiers were slightly

wounded. Inspector Pickup had suffered the indignity of
a neat bullet hole through the centre of his bowler hat.
Mr. Brown, the Spaniard, and two of his men, were
apparently none of them hurt. They stood now in a
group at the end of the drawing room whilst a young
soldier with a tommy gun regarded them impassively.
His last action had been against German paratroopers in
the Valley of the Santerno. He found his present victims
unimpressive.

Chief Inspector Hazlerigg removed a much folded
paper from his pocket and addressed himself to Mr.
Brown.

"I have here," he began, "a warrant for your arrest
charging you firstly with being concerned in the murder
of Sergeant Pollock then attached to the Special Branch
of the Criminal Investigation Department——"

• 4 •

Four months had gone by.

McCann and Mrs. McCann (formerly Kitty Carter)
were sitting in their private sanctum. The last customer
had yielded to persuasion and gone from the saloon bar
of The Leopard, and the kettle was boiling for their
nightly cup of tea.

Glasgow had left a final edition of the evening paper
on the table and McCann read from it the account of
the double execution of Samuel Garret, alias Samuel
Gilbert, alias William Brown of London, and Ramon
Martinez, late of Seville.

The public had been told surprisingly little of the true
circumstances and their interest tended to be statistical.
As "Jack of London" remarked, in his popular and
widely read column, it was almost exactly twenty years
since two men had together suffered the supreme pen-

alty of the law; by coincidence, on the former occasion also for the murder of a policeman.

"They never caught—what'sit—that kid, did they?" said Mrs. McCann as she threaded the first needle for her nightly, ever-losing battle with Major McCann's socks. "The one who got away on his motor bicycle that night?"

"No," said McCann. "No, they didn't. In fact, even at the trial and afterwards, no one seemed to know his name. It really was rather odd, when you come to think of it. The police witnesses called him 'a youth associated with the prisoners'. The gang called him 'that kid'."

"I don't believe he ever had a name," said Mrs. McCann.